CHASING SUNSETS

RACHEL HANNA

Several years ago, my family went to Pawley's Island, SC for vacation. I'd been wanting to see a sunset over the water for years, but I would always miss it. On this particular trip, we drove all over town trying to find a place to see it. Unfortunately, we missed it that time, but my daughter said something along the lines of, "We spent the whole time chasing sunsets!"

As soon as she said it, I knew it'd be a book title one day. So, here's your dedication, Bailey. :)

CHAPTER 1

e stood on the beach, his toes right at the edge of the water. The foamy waves rippled over his feet as he let out a long sigh. It had been a long three years, and he was glad to have a home base again. Seagrove wasn't a place he'd ever visited, except only in his mind. The pictures he'd seen of the sunrises and sunsets were beautiful, and he was looking forward to seeing them in person.

Tonight, however, the moon was his view. It was a clear night, even though a big storm had blown through just hours ago. The sunset he'd hoped to see on his first night there was blocked by dark clouds and a lightning show unlike any he'd ever seen. In fact, he'd seen those bolts rain down from the sky and hit the nearby lighthouse, a place he wanted to visit as soon as he was settled in.

Three years. That was the length of time he'd been on the road. Of course, what he'd really been doing was running. Running away from life. From grief. From memories.

Now, as he stood in the middle of the dark beach, the sound of the waves lapping at his feet, he was forced to actually *feel* his feelings. Running hadn't eliminated the pain. It was there, like a fresh wound ready to remind him of the past.

He stepped back a few feet and sat down, making sure to keep a safe distance between him and the water. The clothes he was wearing were all he had until his personal belongings arrived from his storage unit. Traveling for three years with a backpack and his paint supplies had meant he didn't get to have a full wardrobe. He had two pairs of pants, two shirts, a pair of now ratty sneakers, and enough underwear to not scare other people away.

In the past three years, he'd been all over the world painting sunsets. Aruba. Bali. Italy. Now, he was finally back in the states and ready to start rebuilding his life, if that was even possible.

Losing his wife of fifteen years was a shock to his system in ways he couldn't put into words. The love he'd shared with Katherine had been deep and abiding. When cancer came and ravaged her body, taking her away only three months after diagnosis, he could barely breathe.

Katherine had been his rock. They'd met in his last year of college, where he'd gotten an art history degree. He'd done nothing with it, of course, choosing instead to live the life of a starving artist for years. His paintings didn't sell well for many years, but Katherine had continued encouraging him while supporting them both with her job as a nurse.

For most of their marriage, they'd lived along the Gulf Coast of Florida. There wasn't a huge art scene there, but people did like buying from local artists. One person who'd purchased from him was Georgia Daynes, the owner of a prominent gallery in Atlanta. Over time, they'd worked out a deal where he supplied her with pieces, and she sold them. It was a great deal for Heath and Katherine, especially as they tried to build their family. They'd waited many years to have children, mainly because Heath wanted them to be financially stable first.

Instead, fate had other plans. When they couldn't get pregnant after over a year of trying, they went to a fertility specialist expecting to be given medication or options for IVF. Instead, the doctor saw something, and it didn't look right. In what seemed like a whirlwind of appointments and tests, Heath marveled at how strong his wife was. He knew she was scared, but she didn't show it.

When the doctor came in after her final round of testing, his face said it all. Heath's heart shattered when he explained that she had stage four ovarian cancer, and the treatment options were limited. It had spread - metastasized he called it - to her liver and beyond. They could "try" chemo, but it would likely make her very sick and not prolong her life. The chances were slim, and they needed to make decisions.

Heath wanted to beg his wife to take the treatments, to do anything and everything they'd let her do. But he knew it wasn't his choice. Everyone had one life, and they got to do with it what they wanted. In the end, Katherine chose no treatments. Being a nurse, she'd seen what some of them did, and she didn't want to experience that as her final weeks or months on earth.

It went fast, which was something he was angry about and thankful for at the same time. No amount of years would've been enough, but three months was definitely too little.

He closed his eyes and sucked in a deep breath of

the sea air. Katherine's favorite place had been the ocean. Any ocean. She didn't care which one. It was probably one of the reasons he'd taken off after her death, intent on spending his evenings on beaches around the world, painting the sunsets she'd never get to see. He liked to believe it was his connection with her.

"You okay, sir?"

Heath was startled by the sound of a young boy behind him. He quickly turned and looked up, the boy's face partially illuminated by moonlight.

"Oh, I'm fine." He wondered if he was on private property or something.

"My mom and dad own that inn over there. The one with the string lights on the deck. I'm Dylan." He reached out his hand to shake Heath's, which struck him as so unusual with kids these days. Most of them didn't know how to look up from their cell phones.

Heath shook his hand and then stood up. "I'm Heath Dutton. I just rented the little red cottage down the road."

Dylan nodded his head. "The one with the dock out back on the marsh?"

"That's the one."

"That's a cool house. I ride my bike down there sometimes."

"Dylan? Are you out here?"

A woman's voice permeated the night air. "Over here, Mom!"

She walked over and smiled, putting her arm around her son's shoulder's. She was probably wondering why he was talking to some strange man on the beach at night.

"Hi. I'm Heath. I just rented the cottage down at the end of the road. Near the lighthouse?"

She nodded. "Nice to meet you Heath. I'm Julie. I guess you've met my son here, who is supposed to be taking a shower right now," she said, looking down at him.

"Sorry," he muttered before running toward the house.

"Nice to meet you, Dylan!" Heath called.

"He's a bit of a scatterbrain, that kid," she said, laughing.

"I was just down here having a quiet moment. I hope you don't think I'm some weirdo talking to kids on the beach at night."

Julie smiled. "No. I'm well aware my son can interrupt a quiet moment very easily. We're all pretty friendly around here. My husband,

Dawson, and I own The Inn at Seagrove over there."

"That's what Dylan said. What a beautiful place you have."

"It's been in my husband's family for many years. I'm blessed to call it home now."

"Well, I don't want to take up any more of your evening."

"Of course. Enjoy the beach as long as you want. That's what it's here for, to heal us." She started walking back toward the inn.

"Hey, Julie?"

She turned around. "Yes?"

"How did you know I need healing?"

She shrugged her shoulders. "We all do."

~

THE ROOM WAS loud as the children ran around screaming. Dawson's eyebrow's knitted together as he looked at his wife. "We should've brought earplugs," he said loudly.

She giggled. "I think this might mean we're getting old."

He shook his head. "In our forties? No. I cannot accept that notion. Take it back."

Julie patted his leg. "It's a blessing to get older, honey."

Their granddaughter, Vivi, ran around with the other kids, twirling and laughing about this and that as Dawson and Julie sat in the audience. The performance would be starting soon, but for now, the kids were just energized by chocolate milk and cookies.

"Dylan said y'all met a new neighbor last night?"

"Oh, yes. His name is Heath, I believe. You know how bad I am with names."

"Yes, I know, sweetie," he said patting her leg. Julie had never been good with names, even of people she'd met several times.

"Anyway, he seemed like a nice guy. Dylan said he's renting the red cottage."

"Oh yeah? That one has a great dock over the marsh. Wonder if he likes to fish?"

She laughed. "You don't have time to fish, Dawson. You're behind on projects as it is."

"That's because my honey-do list keeps getting things added to it, so I can never catch up!"

"Hey, y'all. Thanks for coming. Sorry I'm late," Meg said, rushing over to them, out of breath. She sat down next to Julie and tossed her giant tote bag on the floor.

"Traffic?" Dawson asked, jokingly. Seagrove

never had traffic, unless it was a line of ducks trying to make its way from the pond to the marsh.

"No. I had a job interview, actually. And then Christian called because he forgot his lunch, so I had to take that over to the college."

Julie and Dawson were at Vivi's preschool for grandparents' day, and Meg had decided to meet them there since she was one of the room mothers.

"How'd the interview go?"

Meg smiled. "I got the job!"

"Really? What will you be doing?"

She leaned over to whisper. "I'll be a teaching assistant right here at the preschool. Nobody knows yet."

"Oh, honey, I'm so happy for you! I know you'll be glad to be near Vivi during the day."

"I will, plus I really love helping with the kids. I'm hoping to work my way up to a full-time teaching position."

"That's wonderful, Meg. Congratulations," Dawson said.

"Mommy!" Vivi, as usual, seemed to come from nowhere, almost tackling her mother. She was a strong kid to be so petite.

"Hey, Vivi! How are you doing today?"

"We're gonna sing for all the grandmas and grandpas!"

"I know. Are you going to sing real pretty?"

She put her hands on her hips and rolled her eyes. "I always sing pretty, Mommy!"

And just like that, she was gone again, like the busy little bee she was. Julie loved her spunk. She hoped she kept it her whole life, even when things tried to knock her down.

"That kid," Meg said, laughing. "She keeps me on my toes."

"She keeps all of us on our toes," Julie said, watching as the teacher tried her best to corral all her students onto the little stage at the same time.

"Have you heard from your sister lately?"

"She called me last night and said she and Tucker are coming home soon. She sounded happy."

Colleen and Tucker had been traveling all over the country for their new toy company, and Julie missed them. She was glad to hear Colleen sounded happy, but she selfishly wished they'd stay in Seagrove and stop meandering around the entire United States.

"I'm glad she sounded happy. Maybe they got a big deal with one of the stores they were wooing," Dawson said.

Meg shrugged her shoulders. "I don't know. She was being kind of secretive about it. I guess she wants to tell us the good news when she gets back."

Before they could discuss it any further, the lights dimmed and the children finally lined up on the stage. As the music started, Julie felt a smile spread across her face. She'd enjoyed raising her children, of course, but there was just something about watching her first grandchild sing a song on stage that warmed her heart in a way she couldn't describe.

Grandchildren were gifts from God, and she would never take the time she had being a grandmother for granted.

~

COLLEEN WALKED DOWN THE SIDEWALK, happy to be back in Seagrove after several weeks of traveling. She'd missed her sister, her mother, and everyone else she loved. Still, she had a knot in her stomach over the secret she was keeping.

She thought about when Meg came home pregnant and how hard that must have been for her to tell their mother. She didn't have that kind of news, but her news was still going to be both exciting and crushing to her mom. She didn't know how or when she would tell her, but she needed to do it soon before the anxiety ate her up inside.

"Is that my granddaughter right there?"

She turned to see her grandmother, SuAnn, standing in the doorway of her bakery, Hotcakes. Colleen sure had missed her pound cakes.

"Hey, Grandma!"

SuAnn walked over and hugged her tightly. "I didn't know you were back. Wonder why your momma didn't tell me? I swear I'm always the last to know everything."

"Relax. She doesn't even know I'm back. We drove overnight to get home. Tucker is taking a long nap right now since I slept a lot in the car."

"Well, come on in and have a treat with your old grandma." SuAnn pulled on her arm, and Colleen followed, mainly because she needed a big sugar rush.

"Wow, you painted the place since I left?"

SuAnn walked behind the counter and retrieved a slice of peach pound cake. "Yeah, I had that done last month. Don't you just love the color?" It was a pale seafoam green color, and it really felt beachy now.

"It looks great!"

"Coffee?"

"Of course," Colleen said, laughing. "How's Nick?"

"As peppy as always, of course. He's joined a bowling league," she said, rolling her eyes.

"Did you join, too?"

SuAnn looked at her like she had two heads. "Now, does your grandmother seem like the kind of person who'd join a bowling league? The shirts and shoes alone would keep me from doing such a thing."

She walked over to the table and set the pound cake and coffee in front of Colleen before sitting down.

"How's business?" Colleen asked before taking a sip of her coffee. It was early summer in the Lowcountry. It wasn't terribly hot yet, but she knew the humidity was coming.

"It's steady. I really can't complain. How's your business?"

"We've got some big opportunities with some of the larger stores. Oh, and Tucker is licensing one of his inventions to a major brand."

"Wow, that all sounds so exciting, dear. I'm so happy for the both of you. So…"

"So?"

"When do you think he'll pop the question?"

Colleen shook her head. "I knew you were going to go there. You realize not everyone wants to get married, right?"

"But you do."

"And how do you know that?"

"You're my granddaughter. I know everything about you."

Colleen forced herself not to laugh out loud given that she was keeping a huge secret. "This pound cake tastes different."

"Do you like it?"

"Yes, it's so good. Did you change the recipe?"

SuAnn grinned like a Cheshire cat. "I changed it a few weeks ago, and then I applied for a contest with it."

"A contest? Like the local baking contest again?"

She waved her hand and scoffed. "Oh Lord, no. Way bigger than that!"

"What is it then?"

"Have you heard of Sassy Southern Magazine?"

"Definitely. I read it all the time while we're on the road."

"I won their 'best bakery' award!" SuAnn said, beaming.

"You did? That's amazing, Grandma!" Colleen

reached over and squeezed her hand. "I'm so proud of you."

"Thanks, hon. It'll come out later this month, and I hope it brings a bunch of new people to the bakery."

"I'm sure it will," Colleen said, taking her last bite of pound cake. "Well, I'd better go find Mom and Meg. Let's have lunch soon?" she said before standing up.

SuAnn stood. "Let's do it. Maybe a girls' day out."

"That would be wonderful. I love Tucker, but spending day and night with him alone for weeks on end… well, you know."

Her grandmother laughed. "Honey, men can only be a certain amount of interesting before they become a bit dull. That's why we need girlfriends."

Colleen hugged her. "I've missed you. I'll see you soon."

As she walked out of the bakery and toward the bookstore, Colleen felt so grateful to be home. Being surrounded by everyone who loved her was a gift she knew not everyone was given.

CHAPTER 2

*D*ixie stared at the box sitting on the table. For the life of her, she couldn't remember what she was supposed to do with it. Had she prepared it to be mailed, or was she supposed to open it?

Things like this had been happening to her more and more lately. Even Harry had noticed it, and he rarely noticed anything. Within an instant, she remembered this was a new box of books that was delivered yesterday. Grateful her memory had kicked into gear, she started unpacking the new romance books.

She tried to keep it hidden that her memory seemed to be failing her, but it was often hard when working around Julie, who seemed to notice everything. Julie fussed over her all the time, probably due to her Parkinson's diagnosis, and she appreciated that. But she didn't want to feel old and feeble.

A couple of years ago, she'd seen her doctor about memory issues, and it had turned out to just be a sleep medication side effect. Once she'd stopped taking that medication, her memory issues had subsided. This time, though, she wasn't taking any new medication.

She decided that she wouldn't mention today's little memory hiccup. The next time she went to the doctor, maybe she would say something. As she got older, she found it harder and harder to go to the doctor.

She remembered back in her younger years when she would bring up a concern, and the doctor would wave it away and tell her she was too young to worry about such things. At her age, nobody said that anymore.

"Dixie?"

She turned around to see Colleen standing in the doorway. Somehow lost in thought, she hadn't even heard the door chime.

"Colleen? Oh my goodness! You sure are a sight for sore eyes!" She threw her arms around Colleen's neck and hugged her tightly. Julie's girls were just like her own grandchildren now, much to SuAnn's dismay.

"You look well. I'm so glad to see everybody in Seagrove again. Where's Mom?"

"Oh, she had some errands to run so she left a little early today. She might be back at the inn by now."

Colleen looked over at the counter. "Do you mind if I grab one of those blueberry muffins? I've been craving them for months now."

Dixie smiled. "Of course. Take all you want. I'm just going to take them home to Harry, and Lord knows he doesn't need any more fattening foods. He's put on a good twenty pounds since we got married."

Colleen laughed. She unwrapped the blueberry muffin and popped a piece in her mouth. "So, how's everything been going?"

"Pretty good. Business is a little slow, but you know the time of year makes a difference. Once summer is in full swing, you know we'll be packed with people."

"How are you feeling?"

"Spry as ever!" Dixie said, pasting a smile on her face. The truth was, age did things to the body. No matter how energetic and positive she was, her joints were getting older, and things were starting to tighten up a bit more than she'd like.

"Glad to hear it. I guess I'll head on over to the inn soon. Although, I do need to go wake Tucker before he sleeps the day away."

"Well, darlin', it was good to see you. I hope you'll be staying around for a while?"

Colleen walked toward the door, taking the last bite of the muffin before throwing the cellophane into the trashcan. "I hope so. We've got some big things coming, and I hope Mom will be happy to hear them."

"I'm sure she will. Your mama always supports you girls."

As she watched Colleen leave and walk down the sidewalk, she thought about how much she wished she had given birth to at least one daughter. Julie had become like a daughter to her, of course, but she would've loved to have had the opportunity to raise a strong woman.

At least now she had a granddaughter, and she spent as much time as she could spoiling her rotten even though she was still just an infant. For a moment, Dixie had the terrifying thought that maybe she wouldn't remember her granddaughter one day. Maybe this was all leading somewhere that she didn't want to go. She pushed the thought aside and went back to unpacking the box, determined not to let negative thoughts get her down today.

~

HEATH STOOD in the middle of his new cottage and looked around. This was the most space he'd had had in three years. Even though he and Katherine had owned a nice home in the suburbs, traveling alone for so long meant that he was normally in hotel rooms and sometimes tents.

He wasn't sure how he was going to fill this place up with stuff. He'd have some of his things from storage, but those were mostly personal items. When he'd sold the house three years ago, he had also sold pretty much all of the furniture, except for a couple of pieces that had sentimental value.

One thing he had sold was the bed he shared with his late wife. It was a place where she had taken her final breaths, and he just couldn't bring himself to ever sleep in it again.

So, in the months following her death, he had slept in the guest room until the house sold, and then had a big estate sale.

He did keep their small kitchen table as it held

memories of doing puzzles and playing games of Scrabble. She had always won. He'd insisted that she had cheated in some way, but how does a person cheat at spelling words?

He was mostly looking forward to getting his own clothing, so he had more of a choice of what he wore than the few pieces he had right now.

Grabbing a bag of potato chips he brought from the kitchen counter, he walked out onto the back deck. One of his favorite things about the property was that it overlooked the marsh, and it had a fantastic dock out back where he could fish. He hadn't fished in years.

He stared out over the water, the grass sticking up and blowing in the breeze. It was getting later in the day, and he was looking forward to watching a beautiful sunset right from his own home. He wouldn't paint this one right now, but maybe at some point in the future.

His phone vibrated in his pocket, and he looked down to see that Georgia was texting him. She was begging him for new pieces to put in her gallery. He hadn't sent her anything in several months, despite her repeated requests.

After three years of nonstop painting and traveling, he found himself feeling a little burnt out. He wanted some time off, but he also didn't want to lose the momentum of his business, of course.

Still, he couldn't do it right now. He was in the middle of a move, and he just needed a few days off. Sunsets were beautiful, but he often found that he didn't get to really look at them. He was so focused on getting the colors and the shadows right, but he didn't enjoy them like the people who probably looked at his paintings.

He hadn't enjoyed much of anything since his wife died. At first, there was a level of guilt he felt anytime he found himself smiling or laughing at something funny he read on his phone.

There came a time where he thought about dating again. He looked at those apps, and he swiped and swiped. In the end, there was just nobody that could measure up. Maybe there wasn't another woman out there for him. Maybe she had been the only love of his life, and if that was the case, he was okay with it. After all, some people never got even one true love.

Heath considered himself to be lucky that he'd experienced that once in his life. At only forty-two years old, it was hard to imagine spending the rest of his life alone. Men needed companions more than women, he thought. Still, he wouldn't settle for less than what he'd already had with Katherine. If he couldn't have that kind of deep, abiding love again, he'd rather be alone.

"Knock, knock!" He heard a woman's voice at the front door. Having left the door open with the screen door closed to get a cross breeze, he could easily hear anyone approach.

Heath turned and went back into the house, tossing the bag of chips on the coffee table as he did. He saw Julie and a man he could only assume was her husband.

"Oh, hey there," he said, smiling. Getting used to small town life was going to be interesting. Where he used to live, people didn't show up unannounced at your door unless they were trying to sell you something.

"Sorry to bother you, but we have to welcome new people to the island with some kind of treat. Hope you like banana bread?" Her warm smile was comforting. It reminded him of Katherine and the way that she was always able to make other people feel at ease. He missed her, but even more he missed having someone smile at him like that.

"I love banana bread. Thank you," he said, taking it from her hand.

"Oh, this is my husband, Dawson," she said,

smiling up at him. He was a tall guy and had what most would describe as broad shoulders. Heath wasn't quite as tall as him, so he also had to look up a bit.

"Nice to meet you, Dawson," he said, reaching out to shake his hand. "I'm Heath Dutton."

"Welcome to Seagrove," Dawson said, smiling. "We can always use more men around here."

Heath laughed. It had been years since he'd had a group of male friends. Moving around all the time hadn't lent itself well to making friends.

"Would y'all like to come in? I mean, I don't have any furniture inside just yet, but I do have a patio set out back."

"We don't want to impose," Julie said.

He laughed. "Listen, I could use the company. I've been traveling alone for three years."

Her eyes widened. "Really? Well, then, I need to hear this story."

They followed him out back and sat down at the small table. "Wow, this is a great view. I've always loved that dock," Dawson said, staring out over the water.

"Yeah, it was the main reason I chose this place. Well, that and it was the only one available for rent," Heath said, laughing.

"Do you like to fish?"

"I love it. I haven't done in in years, though. Kind of weird because I've been traveling to beaches all over the world for three years, and I haven't fished once."

"Three years? What do you do for a living?" Julie asked.

"I'm an artist. I paint sunsets."

"Oh wow! What a unique job to have."

"I enjoy it a lot. Traveling for three years straight was exhausting, though."

"Why were you gone so long?"

"Honey, the man just met us. Maybe he doesn't want to tell us his life story right now," Dawson said, putting his had on her knee.

She looked at him apologetically. "I'm so sorry, Heath. I tend to ask a lot of questions. I don't want to intrude."

He chuckled. "It's fine. I'm an open book kind of guy. My wife passed away a little over three years ago. I needed a fresh start, I guess."

"I'm so sorry for your loss," she said, sadness on her face. "What was her name?"

"Katherine." He held his emotions together, unwilling to burst into tears in front of his new neighbors. Grief was weird. It came in waves, and it didn't RSVP. It just showed up like an unwelcome, uninvited guest at the most inopportune moments. Once, he remembered falling to pieces in the middle of a McDonald's while he was eating French fries. The poor kids in the play area ran straight to their moms. Right now, he needed to change the subject. "So, Julie tells me that you run an inn?"

Dawson nodded. "Yes, it's been in our family for generations. I also do woodworking."

"I bet you get a lot of interesting people coming to the inn."

Julie laughed. "Actually, they're pretty normal. It's our own family and friends that are interesting most of the time."

Heath smiled. "I miss having family and friends around me."

"Do you have any family at all?" Julie asked.

"Extended family. Aunts, cousins, that kind of thing. My parents died years ago. And I didn't have any siblings. Grief often changes how the people around you treat you, unfortunately."

"So no children?"

He shook his head. "No. It was just never in the cards for me and my wife, and then she got sick."

"I'm so sorry. I can't even imagine."

"Have you two been married a long time?"

"Not all that long," she said, looking over at Dawson and smiling. "I had my own checkered past. Divorced after twenty-one years with a husband who had a secret life. It's the stuff novels are made of."

Heath chuckled. "Sounds like it. Kids?"

"Two grown daughters, a granddaughter, and we recently adopted our foster son. He is entering middle school soon."

"Dylan? The one I met on the beach?"

"That's him. He's a handful."

"He seems like a good kid."

"He's a great kid," Dawson said, pride painted on his face. There were times that he was so sad he hadn't had children of his own. Adoption would have been an interesting thought, but as soon as they got around to talking about it, his wife was sick.

It made him upset that he hadn't gotten those moments with his own son or daughter, tossing the ball around in the yard or going to parent events at school. He'd had wonderful parents and had always assumed that he would be a dad one day. At his age, that was very unlikely now.

"So, Julie, do you run the inn, too?"

"I help with it, but I work at the bookstore. Actually, I'm part owner with my friend, Dixie."

"A bookstore? I'll have to go there. I love to read."

"My mother owns the bakery just down the street. Be sure to go by there and try some of her poundcake."

He smiled. "Sounds like a very tight-knit town."

"Seagrove is a family. We take it very seriously around here. When new people show up, we try to show love. I hope you will get plugged in, and find some new family here. That's what happened to me."

"I hope you're right. I really need a new start. It has been hard."

She nodded. "I can't say that I understand what it felt like to lose your spouse, but I can say that Seagrove is a great place to start over. My life has never been the same since the day I arrived here. I never knew that I could have such a big circle of family and friends. When I went through my divorce, I thought my life was over, but it turned out my life was just beginning."

As much as he was still sad, and would always be sad, that he lost his wife, the idea of a new beginning was the only thing that held him together. The thought that he could start over and at least have friends in his life again kept him going. Seagrove was starting to seem like the most likely place that could happen, and for the first time, he felt hopeful about the future.

~

COLLEEN PULLED up in front of the inn, her palms sweaty. After going to the bakery and the bookstore, she went back home to wake Tucker so he didn't sleep all day. Now, as she sat in front of her mother's house, she wondered how she would tell her the news.

The sun was going down, so she took a moment to stare out over the ocean. While they didn't get a direct view of the sunset over the ocean, the colors were still beautiful. The pinks and blues slowly disappeared as the orange color swept across the sky. Then, there would be darkness. Moonlight. Stars.

She closed her eyes and sucked in a long breath, slowly blowing it out. Her aunt Janine had taught her so many breathing exercises, and they'd served her well in times of stress... like right now.

Colleen got out of her car and walked up to the front door. Not wanting to startle her mother, she knocked on the door instead of just walking inside. She couldn't wait to see her after months of being away, and she knew her mom was going to be very excited.

Instead, Lucy opened the door. "Oh, hey, hon! Good to see you. Come on in!"

She followed her inside and sat down on the sofa. "How've you been?"

Lucy smiled. "I've been wonderful, dear. You want some sweet tea? Or some coffee?"

"No, thank you. Are Mom and Dawson here?"

She shook her head. "No. I think they went to meet a new neighbor. I'm still preparing dinner. Do you want to stay and eat?"

Colleen thought for a moment. She was tired, and Tucker was probably sacked out again. Maybe it would be better to tell her tomorrow when she was well rested.

"No. I think I'll just meet up with her tomorrow. Do me a favor and don't tell her I stopped by, okay? I want to surprise her."

Lucy nodded. "Of course. I'm so glad you're back. Your mama is going to be so thrilled."

Colleen stood back up and walked toward the door. "I can't wait to see her. She's my best friend."

She waved goodbye to Lucy and headed toward her car, looking one last time at the ocean. It never got old.

CHAPTER 3

*E*arly morning was Emma's favorite time of the day. She loved her routine. First, make a very strong pot of coffee. Second, make a nice big bowl of oatmeal with blueberries and maple syrup. Third, take her new little rescue pup out for a short walk around the lighthouse.

She had adopted Walter, a terrier mix, just three months ago. Living at the lighthouse, and being on her own in Seagrove, meant that she was alone a lot. Loneliness wasn't good for anybody.

Even though she had friends, mainly Janine being her best one, she found herself spending most of her nights and weekends by herself. There was just something way too sad about a woman in her early forties spending all of her time alone in a lighthouse.

She was afraid one day they would just find her there, frozen in time, having died from sheer boredom.

After all, there wasn't much to keeping up the lighthouse. She gave tours, of course, and they had events there every so often. But most of her other time was spent reading, watching TV, and sitting alone.

After her last relationship ended, Emma hadn't thought much about dating. Her mind had been consumed with what had happened to her on the police force, and how she had to start over. Now, she was feeling like she was ready to date again, but how did a person find somebody in a town as small as Seagrove?

Janine had urged her to try one of those dating apps, but she didn't trust it. She liked to get to know people face-to-face, and swiping through to pick some stranger to sit with at a local restaurant didn't seem like fun at all.

Of course, having been a police officer, she was very security conscious. She didn't know these people or their backgrounds, and she didn't want to get into that kind of a situation. Maybe she was being overly vigilant, but it was the way she was wired.

So, instead of looking for a boyfriend, she had adopted Walter. He was a good companion, and he agreed with everything she said as long as she fed him his favorite bacon flavored cookies.

"Hold your horses, we'll go out in a minute," she said, admonishing him as he stood at the front door waiting to take his walk. This morning, she was running a little bit slower than normal. They had hosted a wedding the day before, and that was always exhausting.

She finished her last couple of bites of oatmeal and gulped down the last few sips of lukewarm coffee. She would make another pot when they got back before she started her day at the lighthouse.

Tours would begin in about an hour, and it was the middle of the week so she didn't expect a large crowd. Thankfully, there were no field trips coming today. As much as she loved children, having thirty or forty of them climbing the circular staircase of the lighthouse wasn't her idea of a good time.

She opened the door and allowed Walter to run around in circles in the parking area before they headed over to the lighthouse. He liked to run around it, sniffing everything he could find before returning to the house. Thankfully, she had trained him to stay away from the waters' edge. She was right on the edge of the marsh and the ocean, and there were things lurking in the marsh that could easily eat Walter in one gulp.

She opened the door to allow Walter back into the house before she returned to the parking lot to pick up a few pieces of trash she had noticed on their walk. It never ceased to amaze her that people, full grown-ups, would throw their empty cups and napkins onto the ground as if some magical custodian was going to come along and pick them up.

She guessed that she was the magical custodian.

As she picked everything up and then took it over to the garbage can next to the lighthouse, she heard footsteps behind her on the gravel pathway coming from the beach. She wasn't supposed to see the first tourists for almost an hour, so it startled her.

She turned slowly and noticed a man walking and taking pictures of the dunes. "Excuse me?" He said nothing and kept taking pictures without noticing her. She walked closer and spoke louder. "Excuse me!"

Finally, he looked up, obviously startled and smiled. It was a nice smile. "Oh my gosh. I'm so sorry if I scared you."

"You didn't," she said, lying slightly. "You're not supposed to be over here."

"On the beach?"

"Actually, you're on the pathway to the lighthouse. This path is closed to the public."

He looked around and then back at her. "I didn't see any signs."

"Well, there aren't any signs."

"Then how is a person supposed to know?"

She had no good answer for that. "Now you know." She turned and walked back toward the lighthouse.

"Hey!"

Emma turned and looked back at him. "Yeah?"

"Are you the lighthouse keeper?"

"I am."

"Can I take a tour?"

She sighed. "We open in forty-one minutes."

He nodded. "Got it. I'll be back."

"Sounds like a plan," she muttered, before walking back to the house.

∾

JANINE CUDDLED her daughter close as she sat in the rocking chair on her back porch. There were no sweeter moments than those early morning hours when it was just her and Madison, rocking away as they looked out over the marsh.

She loved sharing those moments with her new daughter. The sounds and smells of the marsh would forever be emblazoned in her daughter's heart. The Lowcountry had a way of working its way into a person's soul. It had certainly done that for Janine when she'd arrived there.

Sometimes, she allowed herself to think about all the ways her life had changed since she'd shown up on her sister's doorstep. It seemed like a lifetime ago now, but it really hadn't been all that long. Now she sat in her rocking chair as a wife and mother. She had a great relationship with her mother and sister. She had a thriving business doing something she loved. It was almost surreal. She was grateful beyond measure.

Madison cooed in her arms as Janine stared at her little fingers and toes. Becoming a mother had been such a blessing and unexpected surprise. Things never happened quite like you thought they would.

"How are my girls this morning?" William asked, stepping out onto the porch with an insulated mug of coffee in his hand. He kissed Janine on the top of

her head and then did the same to Madison. Seeing
him as a father had given Janine a whole new level of
love for him, if that was even possible.

"A little tired since Miss Priss decided to stay up
all night learning how to use her voice. She's going
to be a strong-willed woman."

"Just like her mother," he said, smiling as he sat
down in the rocking chair next to her. She dreamed
that this was the way they'd always be - sitting
beside each other on the porch in their rocking
chairs, first with their daughter and then one day
with grandchildren. It was a wonderful thought.

"Heading to work?"

"Yeah. I've got a tour of the marsh with a group
of college roommates today. Four guys who've been
friends for almost forty years."

"Wow! That should be fun." She loved that
William adored his job so much. When she'd first
met him, he was miserable, but since he started his
boat tour business, he left each day with a smile and
came home the same way. Plus, he made his own
schedule, which meant Madison always had her dad
around.

"You need anything before I go?"

"Mind putting another pot of coffee on before
you go?"

"Sure," he said, standing up. "I won't be late today. It's my only tour. Should I grab dinner to bring home?"

"Oh, that would be good. How about pizza?"

"Easy and cheap. I love it!"

Janine laughed. "I don't know that I'd go around town telling people you like stuff that's easy and cheap, honey."

"Do you have any classes today?" Janine had been taking Madison to work with her since she was six weeks old. She had a nursery room all set up, and her assistant at the studio watched her during classes.

"I have one around lunch time, and another one at two. Then, we will do some grocery shopping and come home for bath time."

"I'll try to shoot by the studio around lunchtime to see my girls," he said, kissing each of them again. "Gotta run! I'll put the coffee on! Love you!" he said, as he trotted back into the house.

"Love you, too!" she called back. Janine loved the ease of their life together. Each of them were happy in their careers, and they were both thrilled to be parents. "Oh, you know what else we can do today, Maddie girl? We can go see the lighthouse."

~

EMMA UNLOCKED the lighthouse and waited for the first visitors to arrive. She wondered if the good-looking, strange guy from the path was actually going to show up. Part of her hoped he did.

She was happy to see Janine walking up with Madison strapped to her front. "Hey! I didn't expect to see you lovely ladies this morning."

"I thought we'd surprise you," Janine said, giving her a quick side hug.

"I'm so glad. I feel like I haven't seen you in forever."

"I'm sorry. Being a new mom at my age is even more exhausting than I thought it would be."

Janine was a few years older than her, but it still made Emma think about the fact that she'd never had kids. She wanted them, but time was ticking. At least she had genetics on her side. She remembered her aunt had a baby when she was fifty-years-old.

"No need to apologize. I've just missed you. I plan to come to class again soon."

Janine tilted her head to the side. "And how many times have you promised that?"

Emma laughed. "I'll come. I promise!"

"Anyway, we need two tickets to the top," Janine said, looking up at the lighthouse.

"Come on now, you know I'm not charging you. Get up there!" She pointed behind her.

Janine walked past her and through the doorway. "Okay, but that just means your next class is free!"

Emma laughed as she watched her go up the first few stairs, and then turned back around. She was now face to face with the guy from earlier in the morning.

"Oh my gosh, you scared me!" she said, putting her hand over her chest.

He smiled slightly. "I seem to have a knack for that this morning."

"One ticket?"

"Yes, please." He pulled cash from his wallet, and Emma couldn't shake that he seemed familiar to her for some reason. Maybe she'd arrested him in the past.

"Are you visiting Seagrove?"

"Kind of. I'm renting a cabin down the road."

"Oh, a new neighbor then?"

"Yes. What's your name?"

"Emma."

"I'm Heath. It's nice to meet you, Emma," he said, shaking her hand. His hand was large and warm, and she had a little trouble letting it go. It had been a long time since a man held her hand.

His name even sounded familiar. It wasn't like Heath was a super common name. Where did she know him from?

"You can go on up."

He paused for a moment like he wanted to say something, but then nodded and walked away. After a few moments, Emma followed. She liked to give facts at the top of the lighthouse. Janine had heard them a million times, but Heath needed to hear them.

She arrived at the top of the spiral staircase to see Janine and Madison on one side looking out over the ocean while Heath was staring down at the marsh. He looked lost in thought, but she still had to do her job as a tour guide so she walked closer.

"How much do you know about our area?"

Slightly startled, he turned around. "Not a whole lot. I just got to town a couple of days ago. I plan to do some sightseeing, read up on my new hometown."

"Do you plan to stay here long-term?"

"I suppose it depends on how things go really. I hope I like it because I'm looking for a new start."

That was mysterious. She wondered why he

needed a new start. Had he just gotten out of prison? Sometimes her former job made her think things were a little darker than they probably were.

"I came here for a new start also. It's a great place. I think you'll really like it."

"Mind if I ask why you were starting over?"

"Yes, I do mind. Now, would you like to know some facts about the lighthouse?"

He smiled slightly, probably annoyed by her snappy comeback. "Of course, I'd love to know some facts about the lighthouse."

She turned and looked out over the water, trying not to make eye contact with him. There was just something that she couldn't put her finger on that made her want to stare at him, and that wasn't what she was planning to do.

"The lighthouse was built in eighteen twenty-seven, but renovations were done a few decades later because it sustained some damage."

"Hurricane, I suppose?"

She nodded. "Yes, definitely a hazard around here. Especially on this little island. But we take care of each other, and we heed the warnings when they come."

"Technology is a wonderful thing. Back in those

days, they couldn't have possibly known when a hurricane of that magnitude was coming."

"We also had more damage in eighteen eighty-six after the Charleston earthquake."

"I'll have to look into that. I love to read and research. I guess you could say it's a hobby of mine. I've loved history since I was a kid."

"Me too, honestly. I used to be in the history club in elementary school. Only the biggest nerds were in there."

He laughed. "We have that in common. I don't think I've ever met anyone else who was in history club from that young of an age. I remember my grandparents giving me their old set of encyclopedias for Christmas one year."

"Kids don't know what they're missing out on these days not getting to read those hardback encyclopedias. We had a set also. My parents told me they paid a lot of money for them."

Heath laughed. "We sound like a couple of old people. Talking about things back in the good old days. Wishing we still had rotary phones and no Internet."

She waved her hand. "I don't think I'd go that far."

"What's all the laughing over here?" Janine asked, walking closer.

"We are just talking about the good old days of rotary phones and hardback encyclopedias."

Janine shook her head. "No, thank you. I'll take my expensive coffee drinks and high-tech cell phone. Let's leave the past in the past, people," she said, laughing.

"Hi, I'm Heath. I just moved onto the island a couple of days ago. Wanted to come check out the lighthouse since it's just a few steps from my new house."

"I'm Janine. You might've already met my sister, Julie? She and her husband own the inn on the island."

"Oh, that's your sister? She came by and brought some banana bread. Very nice couple."

"Yeah, they're great. Well, welcome to Seagrove. I run the yoga studio, so if you ever want to come and take a class…"

Emma pointed at Janine. "Stop trying to recruit everybody to take yoga."

"Actually, I've taken some classes before. I've been traveling around the world for the last three years, so I've ended up in some interesting places. My favorite yoga class was in Bali."

"Wow, Bali? So you're a world traveler?" Emma asked.

"Actually, I'm an artist. A painter. I was traveling around the world for the last three years painting sunsets, mostly on beaches."

She had never heard something quite as interesting as that. Traveling around the world to paint sunsets sounded so romantic and adventurous.

"That's amazing. I've been to Bali. It's a beautiful place," Janine said. "Well, I hate to run, but I need to get back to teach a class before lunchtime. The invitation is open if you'd ever like to come to the studio."

"Thank you. I'll definitely take you up on that."

Janine quickly hugged Emma and then headed back down the spiral staircase with Madison attached to her.

"She's really sweet. We've become good friends since I moved here."

"I'm looking forward to building some friendships again. It's kind of hard to do that when you've been away from people for so long."

"No kids?"

"No. You?"

She shook her head. "No, unfortunately. Life takes different turns than you expect sometimes."

"Very true. I really love this marshland. I've seen a lot of oceans, but not a lot of marsh."

"We have over two-hundred species of birds in our marshes." She didn't know why she shared such a random and uninteresting fact with him.

"I've heard there are boat tours?"

"Yeah. In fact, Janine's husband owns a boat tour company. He can take you through the marsh."

"Have you gone?"

"No, actually I haven't. I plan to."

"Maybe we can go together?"

Suddenly, her stomach clenched. "Together?"

"Well, I know very few people in town. I know a married couple and a woman with a baby, and that's pretty much it. So, I thought that maybe we could be friends? I mean, we are neighbors."

She paused for a long moment. Maybe this guy really just needed a friend. He didn't seem to be a psychopath on the surface. Of course, all good psychopaths were really adept at hiding that fact. Otherwise, nobody would want to be around them.

"Sure. I think I would enjoy that."

"Good. Hand me your phone."

"Excuse me?"

"I was going to program my number into your contacts," he said, furrowing his eyebrows like he was confused about why she seemed so suspicious of him.

"Oh. Of course. Here you go."

He typed his name and phone number into her phone. "When you have some time, shoot me a text. I'm pretty much open any time."

He handed her back the phone. "Okay. I'll do that. Maybe sometime next week."

She went back to telling him some more facts about the island, the lighthouse, and the surrounding area. She found him very easy to talk to, and that feeling of familiarity still nagged at her. Where did she know this guy from? Or was she just totally imagining it because he was so handsome?

~

COLLEEN WALKED DOWN THE SIDEWALK, determined to talk to her mother about the big secret she was keeping. She had already verified that Julie was working, so she just had to summon the courage to go into the store and tell her the truth.

As she entered, she saw Dixie sitting at the table picking at a muffin. Normally, Dixie was up and about doing all kinds of things in the store, but she looked a little lost in thought.

"Hey, Dixie. Is my mom here?"

She smiled slightly. "Yes, honey. She just ran to the back for a minute."

"Are you okay?"

Dixie waved her hand. "Of course. Just a little tired is all."

"Oh my good Lord! Colleen?" Julie dropped a box of books on the floor and ran straight for her daughter, flinging her arms around her neck. "When did you get back?"

"A couple of days ago. I've been chasing you around town but you're never where you're supposed to be."

"Well nobody told me!"

"It doesn't matter now. I'm just so glad to see you."

"I'm glad to see you, too. Here, have a seat."

"I'm going to let you ladies talk and go home a little early today, if you don't mind?"

Julie looked at Dixie carefully. "Sure, go on home. Do you need anything?"

"No, darlin'. I'm fine. As I was explaining to your daughter, getting old is for the birds. I'm a little tired, so I need to put my feet up."

Julie squeezed her hand as she stood up. She watched as Dixie walked out the door.

"I hope she's okay. She's been awfully tired lately."

"I'm sure she'll tell her doctor," Colleen said.

"I am so glad to see your face again. Tell me you're not leaving on any more trips anytime soon."

Colleen laughed. "Not as far as I know. We've just been very busy. Lots of interest in the toys, and Tucker even has some new inventions. Things are going really well."

"I'm so glad, honey. That's all I want for my girls. Happy lives with loving men and successful businesses. What more can a mother ask for?"

"I did want to talk to you about something..."

"Take a look at this!" Before Colleen could continue her sentence, SuAnn came rushing in the door holding a magazine in her hand.

"Mother, you scared me to death! What on earth is wrong with you?" Julie chided.

"I am a full-fledged celebrity!" she proclaimed, slapping the magazine down onto the table in front of her daughter. "Take a look at that."

Julie opened the magazine and looked through it, noticing her mother's article and recipe. Her eyes widened. "This is amazing! Congratulations!"

"I wanted to take you ladies out to eat to celebrate. No men! We have to get Meg first. I've already called her."

"Oh, but Colleen was trying to talk to me about something."

Colleen shook her head. "It can wait. It's no big deal."

"Are you sure?"

"Absolutely! We need to go out and celebrate now that we have a real celebrity in the family!"

As Julie finished her work and gathered her things, Colleen made small talk with her grandmother. Her head was swimming, though, because she wanted to tell her mom the truth. She wanted to get it over with.

CHAPTER 4

"*Y*ou still haven't told her?" Tucker asked as he tied his sneakers. After recuperating from all their travels, he was going back to work today.

"I keep missing her or getting interrupted. I just need to get a few minutes alone with her." She drank her cup of coffee and stared out the kitchen window at the birds flying over the marsh.

Tucker walked up behind her and slid his arms around her waist, resting his chin on her shoulder. "Honey, you have to find a way. I don't feel right about this."

"I don't either. She's going to be so upset."

He stepped back and leaned against the counter. "Do you really think so?"

"I know so."

"Do you think we made a mistake?"

She turned and looked at him, putting her hand on his cheek. "Of course not."

His phone vibrated on the counter. "That's Peter. We have a video meeting in fifteen minutes."

"Go on."

"You sure?"

She leaned in and kissed him softly. "I'm sure."

"I'll try to meet you for lunch," he said, as he grabbed his phone and quickly ran out of the house.

Colleen was so happy to have a man like Tucker in her life. Many women never got as lucky as she had finding a chivalrous, protective, fun man.

She started tidying up the kitchen before she was going to head off to run some errands. She heard a knock at the front door and walked over to see who it was. Surprisingly, it was her sister standing there, smiling and waving through the glass.

"Hey, sis! Is everything okay?" Colleen asked, as she opened the door.

Meg looked at her, confused. "Of course. Why wouldn't everything be okay?"

"Well, you rarely just show up here unannounced."

"Are you busy?"

"No. Come on in." She stepped back, allowing Meg to enter, and then closed the door behind her. Meg followed her into the kitchen and sat at the breakfast bar.

"Where is Tucker?"

"He just left a few minutes ago. I was cleaning up a bit before I go run some errands.

"Well, I wanted to catch up with you. I feel like we've both been running around in circles since you got home."

"Coffee?"

"Always."

Colleen put more water in the pot along with some fresh grounds and pressed start. "Yeah, it's been super busy since I got back. Just trying to catch up with Mom has been impossible. Every time I sit down to have a conversation with her, we get interrupted."

"Is everything good?"

Colleen smiled slightly. "Why are you asking me that? Did Mom send you over here to question me?"

Meg's eyebrows furrowed. "What is going on with you?"

She sighed and leaned against the counter. "I guess I'm just a little tired."

"And skeptical. What are you keeping from me?"

"Nothing. How's everything going with you and Christian?"

Meg laughed and wagged her finger in front of her sister's face. "Oh, no you don't. You're not going to change the subject on me that easily. What secret are you keeping?"

Colleen rolled her eyes. "Why do you think I'm keeping a secret?"

"Because you're my sister, and I've known you my whole life. You have a certain face you make when you're keeping a secret. You'd be a terrible poker player."

The thought made Colleen laugh. She had tried to play poker once in college, and she'd lost miserably. Her roommate had told her to never play again or she would lose everything in her bank account.

"Well, you're wrong this time. I'm not keeping a secret. I've just got a lot going on."

Meg looked at her, knowing she was lying, but let it go for the time being. "One of the main reasons I came over here was to tell you that Aunt Janine invited us to a yoga class tomorrow night. Abigail and Celeste will be there, and I think Emma."

"I'll consider it. I know Tucker and I have a late video call that day."

Meg reached across the counter and squeezed

her sister's hand. "Take some time for yourself. You've been working so hard for the last couple of years. Come to class."

She paused for a moment and then blew out of breath. "Fine. I'll come. What time?"

"Seven. And we're going to do a little girl chatting after that, so plan to stay a little while. Janine said there will be wine."

"Is Mom coming?"

"No. She has to run the store."

What a relief, Colleen thought. She loved her mother and wanted to see her, of course, but until she could tell her the big secret she was keeping, she didn't want to be stuck in a crowd of people with her.

"So, how is everything going with you and Christian?"

"Great. Wonderful. Busy, as usual. I got a new job."

"Really? Tell me all about it!"

As Meg regaled her with the details of her new job, Colleen felt so happy to be home and to have a sister who had been her best friend her whole life. She hated keeping such a big secret from her, but her mother needed to be the first person she told. The question was, when?

~

Dixie sat nervously on the edge of the table, the paper crinkling underneath her as she fidgeted. She had always been fidgety. Always antsy. Her mother used to say she had ants in her pants, and nothing much had changed even now that she was in her seventies.

Why was it that doctors took so long to come into the room when you had an appointment? Yet, if you were late even by a few minutes, they forced you to reschedule. Something about that seemed inherently unfair. These were the thoughts that plagued her as she waited for Dr. Knox to come into the room.

She had just started seeing Dr. Knox a few months ago. Her old neurologist had retired or moved or something. Dixie couldn't quite remember what. And that was part of the reason she was there. She was concerned enough about her memory issues that she made an appointment as quickly as possible.

"Sorry to keep you waiting so long," Dr. Knox said as she came into the room. She sat down on a little rolling stool and smiled up at Dixie. She was a nice enough lady, and she seemed to be very well informed. When Dixie had first met her, she was

surprised at how young she was, but Julie had
reminded her that younger doctors often had more
knowledge because they had just come out of school
and learned the latest and greatest techniques and
studies.

"No problem."

"So, my nurse tells me that you're here with some
concerns about your memory?"

"Yes. Better safe than sorry so I decided to come
on in and see you."

"Okay, but before we get on with that, why don't
we do some of the basic tests we usually do at your
appointments?"

"All right."

For the next several minutes, Dixie ran through
all of the things she normally did at a neurology
appointment. The thing where they had her open
and close her hand as fast as possible. That thing
where they had her slap her palm on her upper thigh
up and down, up and down. Then the doctor
checked her strength by pulling and pushing on her
legs and arms a million different ways. Finally, she
had her walk up and down the hallway to check to
see whether she was dragging her foot or not
swinging an arm.

There were all kinds of things the doctor looked

for now that she had been diagnosed with Parkinson's. Thankfully, medication had kept her pretty stable, and she felt good considering she had a degenerative disease.

There was always that little part of her that worried at each doctor's appointment that this was going to be the time the doctor told her things were taking a turn. Parkinson's was a slow disease for most people, but there were the few that had a much faster decline. Dixie was hoping that she would outlive her Parkinson's instead of it taking control of her life in her later years.

"Everything looks very stable since your last appointment. How do you feel your medicine is doing?"

"Very well. I mean, I hate having to take it so many times a day, but if it keeps me in good stead, I can't really complain."

That was one of the most surprising parts of having Parkinson's that she hadn't realized before. She had to take a certain kind of medication multiple times throughout the day or else it would wear off and she would freeze up. Or her tremors would come back. As long as she took it on time, she did well. Managing her own medication along with her husband's was often a challenge.

"I'm glad to hear it. We won't change anything with your medication then. So, tell me more about these issues with your memory."

"Well, I can't decide whether it's just aging or I'm starting to have dementia. My grandmother had that, and it was a horrible thing for the family. I don't want to do that to my children or grandchildren, or even my husband."

"What kind of symptoms are you noticing?"

"Well, I'll forget what I'm doing right in the middle of doing it. Like the other day, I was on the computer getting ready to type something, and I just totally forgot what it was. It took me a couple of minutes to remember."

Dr. Knox smiled. "You know, I'm only in my thirties, and that happens to me quite a bit."

Dixie smiled and nodded, happy that her doctor was trying to make her feel less afraid, but it wasn't working. "I think mine is a little more concerning. I lose my keys all the time, and sometimes I'm at work and I forget what I'm doing while I'm doing it."

"There are some other tests that we can do, and even some psychological testing. But it sounds to me like you might be experiencing something called mild cognitive impairment."

"What's that?"

"A lot of people get this as they age. It can cause issues with memory as well as following instructions or planning. There is no particular diagnostic test for this, unfortunately. But like I said, we can do some psychological and mental testing to see if it might be that."

"And then what? What happens if I do have it?"

"It's not the end of the world. And it doesn't necessarily mean you're going to get dementia or Alzheimer's. It just means that you might need to slow down a bit. It could be that you're keeping too much of a stressful schedule. It could be that you need to start doing more exercise, eating right, doing puzzles and things like that to keep your mind sharp."

Dixie thought about what she said. Still working at the bookstore and being involved in so many things in town did create more stress for her than it did in the past. Maybe she was going to have to make some changes in her life.

"So you don't think I have Alzheimer's?"

"No, I don't. I don't see any signs of that from what you're telling me. But we will keep a close eye on it, of course. My nurse can do some of those tests with you right now if you'd like."

"Absolutely. I just want an answer so that I can stop worrying about it."

Dr. Knox stood up. "I'll get Carmela to come in here in just a few minutes. It's really going to be okay, Dixie. I truly believe that."

As she walked out, Dixie felt her eyes well with tears. Was it going to be okay? This aging thing was for the birds, she thought. Why couldn't she just stay young forever?

❧

HEATH WAS BOUND and determined to get to know his new hometown. Hopefully he liked Seagrove enough that he could buy a house there in the next couple of years. It was hard to think about putting down roots again without his late wife.

He walked down the sidewalk, looking back-and-forth at all of the different businesses. He saw a barber shop, a dry cleaners, a gift shop. Then he turned his head to the left and saw the bookstore. He loved to read. It was one of his favorite things to do, in fact. Painting and reading.

When he was a kid, people often made fun of him for spending all of his time doing those two things.

He had definitely been a nerd, complete with the glasses and little leather briefcase. Thankfully, he wore contacts now, and his best friend tossed his briefcase in high school for fear he'd never meet a girl.

He opened the door to Down Yonder Bookstore, a little chime dinging loudly as he entered. Julie was sitting at a small round table, and looked up immediately.

"Heath! I'm so glad you decided to come check out the bookstore. Are you looking for anything in particular?"

He shook his head. "No. I was just checking out the town, and I can never walk past a bookstore without going inside."

"Same here."

"What are you working on there?" Julie had a bunch of pink and red papers spread out in front of her.

"Right now, I'm making signs for the Summer Kickoff festival."

"You have a festival just to welcome summer?"

"Are you making fun of us?" she asked, laughing

"Not at all. I've just never heard of that before. Are you on the town council or something?"

"Not officially, but I do a lot of things to help out

with the events in town. Plus, it's good for business. I do hope you'll come to the festival."

He chuckled. "I think to go to a Summer Kickoff festival, you need a date. And right now I am pretty dateless."

"I don't think that will last too long around here. A nice eligible bachelor moved to town. Women will be lining up outside your door."

The thought of that made him nervous. It wasn't that he didn't want to date at some point, but to have to meet women and choose someone to date seemed like a lot of pressure.

"Where is your history section?"

"Straight back there and to the left. It's not huge, but there are some good books."

He nodded. "Thanks."

As he walked back to the history section, he looked at some of the other areas. There was a section for gardening, cooking, romance books. It wasn't a huge store, but they seemed to have a good selection.

He stood in front of the history section looking at all the options. World War I, World War II, the Civil War. He'd read a lot on all of those. He picked one up about World War II and started thumbing through it, looking at all of the pictures. Something about studying history had always brought him peace.

"Great minds think alike," he heard a woman say. He turned to see Emma from the lighthouse standing behind him.

"Are you stalking me?" he joked.

"You wish. Actually, I came here to get a cookbook."

"Do you like to cook?"

She laughed. "Not a lot. I mean, I live alone so there's not much need to be cooking big meals. But, I've decided that I need something to do. Most of the time I'm bored out of my mind, so I thought I'd teach myself to cook."

"That's something I need to do. I was married for many years, and then I traveled alone for the last three, so I've never taken the time to learn to cook."

"You should do it. We can compare notes."

He put the book on World War II back on the shelf and turned around. "I've got a crazy idea."

"What?"

"Why don't we do it together?"

She stared at him. "What? Cook together?"

"I mean, we don't have to do it every night. But we live a few steps from each other, and we both want to learn the same thing. We could trade off.

Cook one night at your house, one night at my house. I bet we could learn a lot that way."

"It would make us more marketable to the opposite sex."

He couldn't tell if she was joking or not. "Yeah, I guess that's a plus."

"I can't believe I'm going to say yes to this."

He smiled. "I can't believe you are either."

"You're not like an axe murderer or anything, are you?"

"Not to my knowledge."

"Okay, fine. What about we start the day after tomorrow?"

"What's wrong with tomorrow? Do you have big plans?"

"Actually, I'm going to a yoga class tomorrow night."

"Interesting."

"No men invited."

"That's fine. I don't want to come to your stinking yoga class, anyway," he said, laughing.

"So, the day after tomorrow, six o'clock at my house."

"Sounds good."

She turned to walk away. "Oh, and we're cooking

something out of this book. Maybe chicken and dumplings?"

"I love chicken and dumplings. Do you want me to get the ingredients?"

"Sure. I'll text them to you."

He watched her walk up to the register and check out, and something inside of him felt weird. Was this a date? Had he just arranged a series of dates with his new neighbor?

CHAPTER 5

*E*mma was excited to hang out with her girlfriends for a night. Janine had invited her to a yoga class, and she knew Abigail, Celeste, Colleen and Meg would also be there.

She decided to arrive a little bit early so that she could change her clothes before class. She didn't want to walk around on the streets of Seagrove wearing her yoga pants. Not that other people didn't do that, but she didn't feel as comfortable in her body lately after spending most of her time sitting around eating potato chips by herself.

When she opened the door to the studio, she was shocked to run smack dab into Heath. He was slightly sweaty, although it was pretty attractive if she was being honest with herself. Wearing a light gray T-shirt and a pair of navy blue gym shorts, he dabbed at his forehead with a small towel.

"What are you doing here?" she asked him, sounding a little too accusatory.

He smiled slightly, dimples appearing on both his cheeks and causing her to have butterflies in her stomach. "Namaste to you, too."

She couldn't remember what Namaste meant although Janine had told her several thousand times. "The question remains, what are you doing here?"

"I came to a class. I told you that I like yoga."

"Wouldn't be because you found out I was coming to class tonight, would it?"

"Are you insinuating that I'm trying to come see you at different places? That doesn't make much sense given the fact that we're going to be cooking together."

"Cooking?" Janine said as she appeared beside them.

"It turns out that we both need to hone our skills in the kitchen, so we've decided to learn how to cook together."

Janine's eyebrow raised as she looked at Emma. "Sounds interesting."

"Anyway, thanks for the class, Janine. I really

enjoyed it, and I'm sure I'm going to feel it tomorrow," he said laughing.

"I'm glad you could come. Remember what I said about your hamstrings. Be careful with those. They're pretty tight."

"Noted," he said, saluting her like she was a four-star general. He winked at Emma before leaving and walking down the sidewalk. She stared straight ahead, not wanting to make eye contact with Janine.

"So, *that* was interesting," Janine said, giggling.

"Don't you start." Emma walked past her and went into the bathroom to change. She stood in there for a moment, unable to keep herself from smiling. What was this guy doing to her?

After she changed, she walked back out into the studio. Janine was telling everyone goodbye as her other friends walked in. First, Abigail and Celeste arrived together. Then Meg, then Colleen, who seemed frazzled.

"Ladies night!" Janine proclaimed, holding a bottle of wine up in the air.

"I thought we were doing yoga?" Colleen said, crossing her arms.

Janine laughed. "We are, we are. This is for afterward." She put the bottle into a wine bucket in the corner of the room. "Everybody get your places."

After a few minutes of chatting, everybody rolled out their mats and sat on them. Janine went to the front of the room and started the initial meditation that she usually did before classes.

They went through about thirty minutes of pretty mild yoga, followed by laying on the floor like a dead body for a few minutes. Emma enjoyed it. She enjoyed anything that allowed her to interact with her friends. It had been far too long.

"And when you're ready, you can open your eyes," Janine said at the end. Emma felt like she had been in a coma for the last few minutes. She sat up, rubbed her eyes and stretched her arms high up into the air.

"Is it wine o'clock yet?" Abigail asked. Everyone laughed.

"I do believe it is!" Janine said, standing up and trotting over to the bottle of wine. She popped it open and poured several glasses, setting them on the long table in the back of the room.

Everybody pulled their yoga mats into a circle as Janine went and locked the front door. Thankfully, it had only been the friends in the class, but she certainly didn't want anybody else coming in. She also pulled the big drapes closed so that people walking up and down the sidewalk couldn't see them getting tipsy on wine after their yoga class.

"I even brought a charcuterie board," Meg said, walking out from the break room area. She set it in the middle of the floor, and Emma's mouth started watering. There was nothing she loved more than a good charcuterie board.

"This is fancy," Colleen said, reaching over and taking a cube of cheese.

"Well, we rarely get fancy in Seagrove. We have to do it sometimes," Janine said, laughing as she sat down.

"So, does anybody have any juicy gossip? The life of a young mother isn't the most exciting," Meg said, biting into a piece of ham.

"The only juicy gossip I know about is that there seems to be a certain new eligible bachelor in town, and I believe he's got a thing for our Emma here." Janine winked at her and pulled her knees up to her chest.

Emma glared at her. "And you would be totally wrong. He's just my new neighbor."

Janine cackled with laughter. "Oh please! You two are going to be going to each other's houses to practice cooking. If that's not just a bunch of dates, I don't know what it is!"

Abigail looked at Emma. "You're going to learn how to cook with your new neighbor?"

"It's very innocent. He just moved here, and he doesn't know anybody. And I'm bored out of my mind at the light house. It's not like I've got a full social life because all of my friends have boyfriends."

"And now *you* have a boyfriend!" Janine said, pointing at her.

Emma knew they were just poking fun at her, but for some reason she was feeling very attacked. Maybe it was because she had been single for so long. Everybody else had partnered up a long time ago, and she was still by herself. At the same time, she didn't want to make any bad decisions about who she dated next. The years were flying by, and she still hadn't started a family, a fact that made her sad when she allowed herself to think about it.

"Can we talk about something else?" Emma asked, rolling her eyes.

"Fine. Don't be mad," Janine said, reaching over and squeezing her knee. "What else is going on with you ladies?"

"Well, I got a new job at the preschool," Meg said. Everybody raised their glass of wine and clinked them together.

"Congratulations! You'll get to be with Vivi every day so I'm sure that will be wonderful," Abigail said.

"I don't get it," Celeste blurted out.

"You don't get what?" Abigail asked.

"I don't understand why you'd want to be with your kid all day? That seems like pure torture to me."

Abigail looked at Meg and shook her head. "And thus the reason that Celeste doesn't have any children."

Celeste shrugged her shoulders. "I'm just saying, I've always heard that moms need a break. If you work where your kid goes to school, when do you get a break?"

Meg giggled. "I guess we'll find out."

"Did you all hear that my mother's bakery was featured in a national magazine?" Janine asked.

"No! I bet SuAnn is so excited," Abigail said.

"Oh yes. Of course, she's bragging about it all over town," Janine said, chuckling.

The women continued talking back-and-forth, updating each other on their lives. Even though they had had a little fun at her expense at the beginning, Emma was so happy to be with her friends. She had forgotten how much she needed this.

They finished the wine and almost everything on the charcuterie board before calling it a night. As they all walked outside, Emma told everybody goodbye before she started walking home. She had opted not to drive but to take the walk from the mainland, over the short bridge and onto the island. She loved walking at night, listening to all the different sounds and feeling the ocean breeze on her face.

She had to admit, she was thinking a lot about Heath. Was he interested in her? What was his story? Part of her couldn't stop thinking about him, and there was this feeling like she knew him from somewhere.

Of course, that was impossible, but she still had this feeling of familiarity gnawing at her. Maybe once they started cooking together, she would figure it out.

~

COLLEEN LINGERED AFTER THE CLASS. Everyone else went home, but she stayed around, helping her aunt clean up after their little get together. Janine started flipping off the lights, but Colleen was still standing there.

"Where is Tucker this evening?" Janine asked, as she closed the rest of the blinds.

"Oh, he's probably having dinner with one of his friends. He's been catching up with everybody like I have."

Janine walked behind the counter and picked up her tote bag, flinging it over her shoulder. She stood there for a moment, looking at her niece.

"Are you okay?"

Colleen shrugged her shoulders and sighed, leaning against the counter. "I don't know."

"You know you can tell me if something's wrong."

"I know. But I would feel bad telling you this particular thing before I talked to my mom."

"You remember that your sister told me she was pregnant before she told your mother?" Janine asked, laughing.

"Yes, and I remember my mother did not like that very much."

"True. But when Madison grows up and needs help, I hope that she'll talk to my sister if she needs to. I would never want her to keep something inside that was bothering her."

"I know you're right. It's just that I've been trying to talk to my mom since I came home, but we keep getting interrupted. It's almost comical at this point."

"If you need me, you know I'm here," Janine said, reaching across the counter and touching Colleen's hand.

She knew she shouldn't tell anyone before her

mother, but she just couldn't stand it anymore. She had to tell somebody.

"Tucker and I got married."

Janine's eyes widened so big that Colleen was sure she could've stuck a toothpick between the upper and lower lids.

"You got married?"

"Yes. About six weeks ago."

"But… Why? Are you…"

Colleen laughed. "Pregnant? No. We got married because we are in love with each other."

"But I thought you would want a big wedding? And you didn't even get engaged."

"Well, the engagement and the wedding sort of happened simultaneously."

Janine walked slowly into the yoga studio and pulled two mats into the middle of the floor, patting one across from her. Colleen followed and sat down.

"Tell me the whole story."

"We were in Las Vegas for a toy convention."

Janine threw her head back. "Oh… I get it now. Vegas."

"Tucker had proposed to me a couple of times, and every time I had declined because I wasn't ready. But then I was ready."

"So he proposed in Las Vegas?"

"Yes. Right by some beautiful fountains in front of a hotel whose name I can't remember right now."

"You didn't want to come home and plan a wedding?"

"No. I didn't want a big wedding. I wanted the marriage, but I didn't want the big white dress or all the people staring at me while I stood at the front of the church professing my love to Tucker. We just wanted to be married."

"Colleen, you know we would've planned even a small wedding for you. Something by the ocean."

"I know. And it had nothing to do with not wanting the family to be there or something. We just got swept up in the magic and the romance of our engagement, and we went straight down to one of those little chapels. And you know what?"

"What?"

"It was the most beautiful night of my life. I wouldn't have had it any other way. I just don't know how to tell Mom."

Janine paused for a long moment as the two of them just sat there thinking. She sighed. "I think she's going to get her feelings hurt no matter how you tell her."

"I feel so guilty. I should've told her weeks ago. I know that. But she's so busy, and now she's running around planning the festival. It just seems like there's never a good time."

"You just have to tell her. It's going to be hard, and she might be a little upset. But she loves you, and she'll understand."

"I hope you're right. Even telling you first makes me feel guilty."

"She never has to know that you told me, but I'm glad you did. You seemed awfully upset lately, and now I know why."

"I'm so happy being married to Tucker. It just feels… different."

Janine smiled. "I understand. Trust me. I'd better get home and relieve my husband. I'm sure Madison is ready to eat dinner."

They stood up and started walking toward the door. "Thank you for letting me confide in you."

Janine pulled her into a tight hug. "Any time, kid."

～

DIXIE SAT on the edge of her bed wearing her favorite pink housecoat. She remembered when she was younger, with a much better figure, telling her grandmother that she would never wear such hideous nightgowns.

These days, she loved them. The ones that slipped right over her head and were flowy were her favorite. She liked not having anything tight up on her skin while she was trying to sleep.

Harry was in the bathroom brushing his teeth and doing his nightly routine. She swore it took him longer to get ready to go anywhere or get ready for bed than it did her. She supposed that women had perfected their beauty routine over the years, but men never did.

She heard him tap his toothbrush on the side of the sink, a sure sign that he was about to come into the bedroom. She needed to talk to him, and she had been procrastinating about it all day.

"Did you see that new blue bird that's been flying around in the backyard? I tried to get a picture of it several times this morning, but that little bugger is fast," Harry said, as he walked into the bedroom. He always wore the same pair of blue and white pinstripe pajamas. He had so many pairs of them, she'd lost count.

"No, I can't say that I've seen it. But I'm sure you'll be building a birdhouse for it soon." Since retiring, Harry had taken up woodworking. He made bird houses mostly, and he often sold them at festivals. They didn't need the money, but it gave him something to do. Idle hands and all that.

"Are you okay, honey? You're usually all snug under the covers by now." He sat down beside her at the end of the bed.

"I'm fine. It's just that I need to talk to you about something."

"What's going on?"

She turned slightly and looked at him. He was a handsome man, even in his late seventies with gray, thinning hair. They both had Parkinson's disease, and that presented a lot of challenges that most people would never understand. But so far, they were both still doing well enough to take care of each other, and that was really all she could ask for.

So many of her friends had lost their husbands already, much like she had in her younger years. She was so blessed to have someone to share her life with, and Harry was very good to her.

"I went to the doctor, and she shared with me that I might have something called mild cognitive impairment. The nurse did some testing, and it's looking like that might be the case."

"What does that mean?"

"I don't really know yet. I'm getting a little more forgetful. I was worried it might be dementia or

Alzheimer's, but the doctor doesn't think that's the case."

"Well, that's a relief. I can't imagine how hard that is for families to go through."

"Me too. But the doctor did say that I need to cut back a little bit. Maybe stop working so much. Do a little more exercise and eating right."

"Dixie, you know I've been telling you that for a while now," he said, taking both her hands. "You don't even have to work at all. This is the time in our lives where we shouldn't have to stress about money or having a job."

"You know I love the bookstore."

"And you can go to the bookstore as much as you want. But maybe it's time to start being a customer instead of an employee?"

She would have to think long and hard about that. Julie was like a daughter to her, and leaving the bookstore could put her in a bind. She didn't want to do that either. Dixie had always had a strong sense of responsibility, even as a child. She didn't want to let anybody down or disappoint anyone.

"I don't wanna be an old lady," Dixie said, scooting over and putting her head on his shoulder.

"You'll never be an old lady. You're Dixie! You're full of energy and vitality. But it's okay to stop working when you don't need to work. Use that energy for other things. We said we were gonna travel more, and then we stopped."

"I know, I know. I guess I have put myself under way more stress lately than I've needed. I'm going to work harder on my exercise and eating, and I'll cut back my hours at the store."

"Good. Now let's climb into bed and watch a little TV before we fall asleep."

She stood up and pulled the covers down on her side of the bed as Harry did the same. "You know what? I don't wanna watch TV tonight."

Harry smiled and winked at her. "Well, then, we won't watch TV."

~

SuAnn liked getting to work early in the morning. She and Nick always had the same breakfast, plain bagels with strawberry cream cheese and a big cup of coffee. They would sit out on her patio overlooking the local golf course and talk about their plans for the day.

Then, she'd walk down the sidewalk towards her bakery, ready to feed the morning patrons followed by the lunch crowd. Thankfully, she closed early enough that she could be home to have dinner with Nick. She liked her routine.

This morning, however, she was shaken out of the familiar when she saw a long line of people standing outside of the bakery, most of them holding a magazine in their hands.

She slowly approached them, moving through the crowd like the sea was parting.

"Are y'all here for poundcake?" she asked, surprised.

The line, made up of mostly women and a few children, all nodded their heads and started talking at once. One woman spoke up. "We saw your article in the magazine. We wanted to come give your place a try."

How was she going to feed all these people? Usually she had a little bit of time before any customers came to start making fresh items. Thankfully, she had a few left over from yesterday that she could start with.

"Okay, just give me a minute to get the lights on, and I'll come unlock the door," she said, slipping quickly into the bakery and locking it behind her. She flipped on the lights, put on her apron and then ducked into the back room with her phone.

"Hello?" Meg said on the other end of the phone.

"Oh, honey, I need your help!"

"Grandma, are you okay?" Meg sounded terribly concerned, and SuAnn felt a little bit bad about that.

"Yes, I'm fine. But when I got to work, there were a lot of people all the way down the sidewalk wanting to try my poundcake!"

Meg giggled. "Well, isn't that good?"

"It would be good if I had any help. Today's my day for working alone. Darcy is off, and she's out of town. Do you think you could run over here and help me?"

"Sure. Let me drop Vivi off at preschool, and then I'll be over. You're lucky I haven't started my new job yet."

SuAnn hung up the phone and quickly pulled all of the poundcake she had out of the refrigerator. She started a pot of coffee, and then went to open the door.

Today was going to be a crazy day.

CHAPTER 6

olleen stood outside of the bookstore, ready yet again to talk to her mother about getting married to Tucker. She just wanted to get it over with, and she vowed that this time she was going to tell her no matter what.

"Oh hey, honey! I'm so glad to see you. Janine said the yoga class and get together went really well last night. Did you have fun?"

"Yes. It was great to see everybody again. I had missed having girlfriends to hang around with. What are you doing?"

Julie blew out of breath and laid her forehead on the table momentarily. "I'm trying to come up with a schedule for the festival. All of these people have signed up for tables, and I also have to help make sure we have secured a band."

"A band?"

"Well, it is the big summer festival. The pavilion is going to be covered in hanging twinkle lights, and couples will be able to dance. I suppose you and Tucker can enjoy yourselves. Maybe he'll pop the question," she said, smiling slyly.

Colleen cleared her throat. "That sounds like a lot of fun." This was the perfect opening. All she needed to do now was tell her mother that she had already gotten married and then close her eyes and wait to hear her mother crying or screaming or whatever she was going to do.

"So, how is everything going?"

"Well, I just wanted to…"

As if on cue, Janine flung the door open, holding Madison in her arms. "I'm taking Madison to the ER!"

It wasn't that Colleen didn't care about her baby cousin, but seriously? How many people or situations were going to continue interrupting her telling her mother this big news?

"What? What's wrong?" Julie asked, standing up and running over to her sister.

"She has a fever of one-hundred and one, won't

stop crying, won't eat. William is out on a boat tour. Would you be able to come with me to the ER?"

"Of course. I'll close the store and put a note on the door."

"No, Mom. That's not necessary. I'll watch the store. I've done it before."

"Thanks, Colleen," Janine said, looking down at Madison.

"Let me go grab my purse, and I'll drive us," Julie said, hurrying to the back room.

"Oh no. You were going to tell her, weren't you?" Janine asked, scrunching her face.

Colleen nodded. "But that's okay. Madison is way more important right now."

"I'm so sorry," Janine mouthed as Julie came back to the front.

"Okay, let's go."

"Text me and let me know what's going on!" Colleen yelled after them before they quickly disappeared.

～

TUCKER WAS NERVOUS, perhaps more nervous than he'd ever been in his life. Even though Dawson wasn't Colleen's biological father, she saw him as a father figure. This was especially true since her relationship with her own father had dwindled to almost nothing over the last couple of years.

It wasn't necessarily that she was mad at him because of his infidelity with her mother, even though she was. It was more that he didn't seem to care to have a relationship with his daughters like he once did. Maybe he was embarrassed. Maybe he was just too busy with his other family.

Tucker tried not to think about it too much or else it made him mad. He was happy that Colleen had Dawson, and he felt like it was the right thing to do to go see him.

He hadn't told Colleen what his plan was. He only knew that she was going to see her mother today and give her the news.

Tucker was normally a traditional type of guy, and he always assumed that he would ask permission to marry Colleen before he did it. But the romance had overtaken both of their senses. Still, looking back, he would have it no other way.

So instead of asking for her hand in marriage, he was going to ask Dawson's forgiveness for marrying her without doing all of that traditional stuff in advance. Dawson seemed to be kind of a romantic himself, so hopefully he would understand.

He was thankful that Colleen was finally telling her mother today. She had seemed so determined when she left the house this morning, and it was likely that Julie already knew. He hoped that she took it well.

He pulled up to the inn and got out. Dawson spent most of his time working in his workshop, making all kinds of tables and chairs. It had started as a hobby, but he did it as a side business now. Of course, he also ran the inn, but Lucy handled most of the day-to-day operations.

He walked across the sandy driveway and stood in front of the door to his workshop. He could hear sawing noises inside, and he only hoped that Dawson didn't try to use one of those high powered tools on him when he heard the news.

Before he could knock on the door, Dawson opened it quickly, almost walking right into Tucker.

"Tucker, you scared me to death!" Dawson said, putting his hand on his chest. It wasn't until now that Tucker realized just how tall Dawson was compared to him.

"Sorry. I was just about to knock."

"It's getting a little hot in there. I was going to go sit on the picnic table for a few minutes."

Tucker nodded. "Mind if I join you?"

"Of course not. I'm glad to see you. Seems like you and Colleen were gone forever."

They walked over to the picnic table and sat down on the top of it, staring out at the water behind the house. Tucker thought the inn had one of the most beautiful views in Seagrove.

"We're glad to be back. There's no place like home."

Dawson eyed him carefully. "What's up?"

"What makes you think something is up?"

Dawson smiled slightly. "It's not often that you come over here just to hang out and chat. Something must be going on. Is Colleen okay?"

"She's fine. But I did want to talk to you about something."

"Okay. Shoot."

"Well, Colleen looks at you as a father figure. I mean, her dad has turned out to be a big disappointment."

"To say the least." Everybody knew Dawson had no love lost for Julie's ex.

"So, I think it's pretty clear that I've been wanting to marry Colleen for a long time. And I always planned to come and ask your permission…"

Dawson suddenly stood up and clapped his hands, grinning from ear to ear. "You're going to propose? Oh my gosh, man! That's awesome! Congratulations! Julie is going to be so excited to plan another wedding."

Tucker stared at him, his face looking like a deer in the headlights. He hadn't expected such a strong reaction, and now he was going to have to tell this man that they had already gotten married. He wanted to walk straight out into the ocean and never come back.

"That's not exactly it…"

Dawson looked at him for a moment and slowly sat back down, the smile disappearing from his face.

"What do you mean?"

"We had a toy convention in Las Vegas a few weeks ago. I proposed there."

Dawson sat with that information for a few moments. "I don't understand then. You're asking my permission after you've already proposed?"

"Yes, kind of."

He smiled again. "It's out of order, but I would've said yes anyway. So, yes, you have my permission to ask Colleen to marry you. I know it's all old-fashioned, but I suppose we have to go through the motions."

Tucker bit his bottom lip. "That's not all."

"No?"

"No. You see, we kind of got wrapped up in the romance of the proposal and being in Vegas."

"What does that mean?"

Tucker sucked in a short breath and then blew it out for what seemed like an eternity. Dawson looked confused and irritated all at the same time.

"We got married already."

The level of silent tension that hung in the air seemed to go on forever. Tucker felt like he was frozen in suspended animation.

"Does Julie know?" The question was pointed and heavy.

"I'm not sure. Colleen has tried telling her several times, but keeps getting interrupted. As far as I know, she told her a little bit ago."

Dawson pulled his phone out and looked at the screen. "She hasn't texted. I hope she's okay. That's very big news."

"I know it is."

"Tucker, this is her daughter. How could y'all go and do that without even letting us know?"

"Like I said, we got caught up in the excitement. Afterward, we both felt terrible. But then again, we're married, and we're happy about that. Colleen decided she didn't want the big wedding."

"We didn't have to have a big wedding. You

could've gone to the justice of the peace right there in town. We would've supported anything."

Tucker put his face in his hands, and rested his elbows on his knees.

"I know. We just feel horrible about it."

After a few minutes, Dawson slapped him on the back. "You know what? It's your marriage. I'm happy that you got married. We always want you in the family. I'm just worried about my wife's reaction."

"Me too."

Dawson leaned back, his hands on the table behind him. "Well, I suppose it's just like anything with our wives. Better to just wait and see."

Tucker chuckled. "I'm pretty new at this, but I also think we should take a wait-and-see approach."

∼

JANINE WAS A NERVOUS WRECK, especially without William there to keep her calm. He was out on an extended boat tour with some executives, and he normally didn't look at his phone while he was working.

She had texted him a couple of times, but she didn't expect him to look at it for at least another half hour or so when he brought his customers back to the dock.

A part of her wanted to be mad at him for not looking at his phone more often, but she knew that he had to be fully present to give a tour. He couldn't exactly stop over and over and look at his phone while he was trying to explain the complicated ecosystem of the Lowcountry marshland.

She was happy to have her sister with her, but there was just something about having her husband that she needed right now.

"Any news?" Julie asked as she walked back into the room.

"No, nothing yet. Thanks," she said, as Julie handed her the cup of coffee she had requested. Hospital coffee had improved a lot in the last few years with the brand new coffee bar that was installed in the lobby.

"I'm sure it's going to be fine. I remember when Meg and Colleen were little. They were always getting some kind of virus or illness. Unfortunately, it's a big part of motherhood to watch your kids get sick and nurse them back to health.

"I know it's to be expected, but she is so little," Janine said, staring at Madison's tiny little hand. She was finally asleep, laying on the table in her diaper and one piece pajama outfit. She'd been crying for hours, so Janine was thankful she was getting a little bit of peace.

"I remember Colleen had strep throat one time when she was about five years old. It was horrible. She just grabbed her throat and cried, and there was very little I could do. You would think modern medical science would have come up with cures for all this stuff by now, but I suppose there are more important things in the world."

Janine fidgeted in her chair and she looked up at the table where her daughter lay. "You know, I wasn't sure I'd ever be a mother. And when this little blessing appeared in my life, I couldn't believe she was for me. My very own daughter. At my age, I just didn't think it was a possibility."

"You're not an old lady!" Julie laughed.

"Listen, when everybody else's kids are already out of high school, and you haven't even had one, you start to get a little punchy."

"So sorry to keep you waiting." A nurse walked into the room. "As you can see from the waiting room, we're quite busy with all of these viruses right now."

"But it's almost summer time. I would think this

sort of thing has died down now that the kids are out of school," Janine said.

The woman smiled. "Oh no. Kids are always passing around germs. In the summertime, they have more time to play together. It's not as bad as it is during the winter, but we still have stuff out there."

"What do you think is going on?"

"The intake nurse says that she's got a fever, irritability, not eating?"

"Yes."

"Have you heard any other upper respiratory sounds?"

"She did cough a couple of times this morning, but I didn't hear anything out of the ordinary."

"Her eyes, do they look red?"

"I don't think so… but she hasn't been sleeping, so maybe…" Janine felt very ill-equipped. This was the first time she had to really think about anybody but herself.

"In summertime, we sometimes see some thing called adenovirus. Children might get a high fever, sore throat, upper respiratory symptoms. It can look a lot like strep throat, but we can do an evaluation. Unfortunately, we'll have to wake her up."

"Of course."

"It's going to be a little while. The doctor is tied

up with a couple of patients before you, but hang in there. We won't wake her until the doctor comes in."

The nurse walked out, and Janine sighed. "I don't know if I am cut out for this taking care of little ones when they're sick thing."

Julie laughed. "No mother thinks they're equipped for that. You don't want to see your child sick or in pain."

"I suppose you're right."

Julie's phone vibrated in her pocket, and she looked down. "Dawson is in the waiting room, apparently. Do you mind if I go out there and talk to him for a few minutes?"

"Of course. It's going to be a while. I'll just text you when the doctor comes in."

Julie walked over and hugged Janine. "It's going to be fine. I'll be back soon."

~

JULIE WALKED out into the waiting room, which was full of people. She wished that she had remembered to grab a mask before she left home because she was sure she was going to catch the flu or some kind of unknown virus that they had only seen in pigs before.

Finally, she scanned the room and saw her husband standing over near the door. He smiled and waved.

"I thought I'd never find you," Julie said, as Dawson leaned down and kissed her on the cheek.

"Should we go outside away from this petri dish of bacteria?"

"Yes, please."

They walked outside to a small courtyard area just off the emergency room doors. A lot of family members sat out there while they waited for news. They found a small concrete table and sat down. Dawson, being the thoughtful husband, slid a strawberry smoothie in front of his wife.

"I thought you could use this."

"How did you know? It's been such a stressful day. First, Colleen came by the bookstore, and then I had to run out to come to the ER. Plus all the festival stuff. Just a crazy day."

"So Colleen did come see you?"

"She did."

"How did that go?"

"It went fine. I mean, we didn't get to talk for too long."

"But things are good between you two?"

She was very confused as to why he was asking

her these questions. "Yes, of course. She's my daughter, after all."

He let out a big breath. "I'm so glad to hear that. When Tucker came over today and told me they had gotten married in Vegas, I was really worried you would take it hard."

Julie suddenly felt like she couldn't breathe. It felt like there was a lump the size of a tennis ball sitting in the middle of her throat. "What?"

Dawson's eyes widened as he realized she didn't know. "I thought you said Colleen came and talked to you?"

"She came by the bookstore, but we didn't talk about anything in particular before Janine ran in with Madison."

"Oh my gosh," Dawson put his face in his hands and ran his fingers through his thick hair. "I'm so sorry. I thought you knew."

Julie sat there with her mouth hanging open slightly. She could feel her heart starting to race, and her hands were shaking. Why would her daughter go off and get married and not even invite her to the wedding?

"They got married without even telling me? I don't understand."

"Tucker said they were in Vegas for a convention,

and he popped the question. They got so caught up in the lights and the romance, that they went to a little chapel…"

She put up her hand. "I don't want to hear anymore."

"Julie, Colleen and Tucker feel terrible about it. I mean, they're glad to be married, but they felt very guilty about not telling you."

"She's been back for days."

"She said she's tried to tell you several times, but you keep getting interrupted."

"I don't accept that answer. She could've told me anytime. She could've called me on the phone or sent me a text."

Dawson smiled slightly. "Honey, if she had sent you a text telling you that she got married, do you think you would've handled that any better?"

"I just can't believe this. I have two daughters, and I fully intended to splurge on two weddings. Why would she do this?"

"Listen, it hasn't been that long since you've had a new romance. You know what happens when you get caught up in all the feelings. She didn't do it to harm you. She did it because she was feeling in love and excited."

She stared at him. "So you're taking her side?"

"There are no sides. We're family," he said, reaching over and taking both of her hands. "Do you want this to come between you and Colleen? Is that really what you want to do?"

She sat there for a moment, staring off in space. "No, of course not."

"Give yourself some time to come to terms with it, and then go talk to her. Don't create a wedge between you and your daughter."

She knew he was right, but she hated that. She wanted to be angry, but she knew that Colleen was madly in love with Tucker, and he was good to her. What more could a mother ask for?

~

JANINE HAD NEVER BEEN MORE relieved in her life when the doctor came in and said that her daughter was going to be fine. She felt like her lungs finally opened.

Madison had been diagnosed with adenovirus, and the doctor said most infections were mild and just needed over-the-counter pain medications. Madison would be okay in a few days, and she just needed to watch her a little more closely than normal.

As she was walking out of the hospital, William came speeding up in his truck, parked in a place that wasn't a parking spot, jumped out and ran toward her.

"Is she okay?"

Janine smiled. "She's going to be. She has something called adenovirus, but the doctor said she should be fine."

He blew out of breath. "I was so worried! I didn't get a chance to check my phone until a few minutes ago, but as soon as I saw you were at the hospital, I just took off. I think I ran a couple of red lights. I'm probably going to get some traffic tickets in the mail."

"Why didn't you just call me?"

He looked at her for a moment. "You know, it never even dawned on me. I just knew I had to get to my girls."

His girls. Janine loved when he said that.

"We are going home. Can you drop by the drugstore and get some over-the-counter pain medication for her?"

"Of course. Let me walk you to the car."

"So, have a little gossip to tell you."

"Oh yeah? What's that?"

"Colleen and Tucker got married in Vegas a few weeks ago."

William stopped in his tracks. "What? Does Julie know?"

"She does now because Dawson accidentally told her. He thought Colleen told her earlier today."

"Oh man. I'm sure he feels terrible."

"He does, and Julie is pretty upset. She had a lot of big plans for Colleen's wedding one day. But Colleen didn't have the same plans."

"I hope they work it out. I would hate to see Colleen and Julie at odds."

They got to the car, and William took the baby's carrier and secured it in the car.

"I don't think that will happen. Julie might be upset for a little while, but she loves her daughters."

"Just like I love my daughter. I was so scared something was really wrong," William said, shutting the door.

Janine wrapped her arms around his waist and rested her cheek against his chest as he held her. "I was scared too. I didn't think I was equipped to handle something like this, especially without you."

He pulled away slightly and looked down at her. "You're the strongest woman I know. And you handled it. With grace and ease just like you handle everything else."

"Well, if it's all the same to you, next time I'd prefer if you were with me."

"Oh, trust me, I will be checking my phone every five minutes from now on."

CHAPTER 7

*H*eath was feeling a little nervous. When he asked Emma yesterday if she would go on that boat tour with him today, he had fully expected her to say no. Tell him she was busy or something.

Much to his surprise, she had said yes. Now he stood on the dock waiting for her to show up, and he had an irrational fear that maybe she would stand him up.

Was this a date? He wasn't sure. He just knew he had this feeling that he needed to be around her. He hadn't had that feeling in many years.

Was he ready to start dating? It had been three years, and he had been stuck in a cycle of grief he couldn't seem to escape. It wasn't until now that he even had the inclination to date, so that must've meant something.

But maybe Emma wasn't interested at all. Maybe she was just being a nice neighbor. Maybe he had forgotten what the signs and signals were when a woman was interested in him.

Or maybe he was just really overthinking things because it was too early in the morning.

He met William a few minutes ago when he got there, and they talked about Janine and her yoga classes. Seemed like a nice guy. He was looking for some new friends, so hopefully he and William could hang out together sometime.

Heath often felt awkward. When he was married, he'd been very social, and they had always gone out with friends. Since being on his own, it was like he'd forgotten how to interact with people.

Artists, specifically painters, were typically solitary creatures. He spent most of his time staring off into the distance and painting what he saw, which left little room for human interaction.

"Sorry I'm late! My dog got sick this morning, and I had to clean up…" Emma said as she ran up behind him. "Never mind, the details are better left to your imagination."

"Or maybe I could just not imagine them at all," he said back, laughing.

"Talking about dog poop in the morning? It doesn't seem like a good way to start the day," William joked as he walked up. "You're ready to go?"

"I think so. But first, how's little Madison doing?" Emma asked. Heath wasn't sure what that was about.

"She seems to be doing a little better. Her fever is down."

"That's good to hear."

"Climb on board. You can sit on opposite side or on the same side. Not sure what's going on here," William said, pointing between the two of them and winking.

"He's my new neighbor," Emma said, making it very clear to Heath that she thought of him as a neighbor and nothing else. Message received. Oh well, he didn't exactly know how he felt about her either.

"Welcome to Seagrove," William said, smiling broadly. He pulled his phone from his pocket, sent a quick text, and waited for a response. "Sorry. My daughter was in the ER yesterday, so I'm just checking with my wife to make sure all is well before we set off."

"Of course. Do what you need to do," Heath said.

"I'm starving," Emma whispered.

"You didn't eat breakfast?"

She looked at him like he was crazy. "I told you my dog was sick. Do you think that really increased my appetite?"

Heath chuckled. "I guess not." He leaned over and opened an insulated tote bag. "Here."

She reached out and took the item that was wrapped in plastic. "What's this?"

"I didn't know how long we'd be out, and I thought we might get hungry. That's a blueberry muffin."

She smiled. "Did you make this?"

He shook his head. "I wouldn't put you through that. I bought it at the bakery, plus a couple of sandwiches from the cafe."

Her facial expression changed to something he couldn't read. "Wow. You thought of everything."

Heath shrugged his shoulders. "I try."

"Are you a serial dater?"

"What?"

"I mean, is this in your bag of tricks?"

"My bag of tricks?"

"The things you do to attract women?"

"Trust me, I don't have a bag of tricks, Emma."

"You're a nice-looking single guy who probably dates a lot of women as he moves across the globe."

"Oh, that's what you think?"

"It makes sense, doesn't it?"

He sighed. "Not for me." Heath turned slightly and looked out over the water.

"I'm sorry. Did I offend you? I was just joking around."

He looked back at her. "Were you?"

"Yes, I was. I just don't know your deal."

He crossed his arms. "And I don't know *your deal* either. Do you want to tell me?"

She paused for a moment and bit her lip. "No, not really."

"Then why don't we enjoy this boat tour without making assumptions about each other?"

Emma nodded. "Fair enough."

"Y'all ready to go?" William asked, walking back over to them.

"Absolutely. Is Madison okay?"

"She's doing a lot better. Janine said I am free to drive around the marsh without worrying."

"Perfect," Emma said, smiling. "I can't wait."

Emma had to admit she was enjoying her time with Heath. It had been years since she'd felt this comfortable with a man, and that made her a little scared. Opening her heart was not something she did easily.

She could tell that he had a story, and she wanted to know more. At the same time, she didn't really want to talk about her own story. It was something she tried to put behind her every day. Her time as a police officer had really done a number on her mental health, but she had worked so hard to get to a good place.

"Look at those birds," Emma said.

William started explaining what kind of birds they were and what part they played in the ecosystem of the Lowcountry, but she had to admit she wasn't paying much attention. She was looking at Heath looking at the birds.

He had pretty eyes. A shade of blue that matched the ocean water, but a little bit lighter. And he had longer eyelashes than most men. They almost looked fake, but not feminine. Just nice.

He was in good shape, which was important to her. Even though she sat around eating ice cream and potato chips by herself most of the time lately, she had always been someone who enjoyed physical fitness. Climbing the stairs at the lighthouse all the time was just about the only exercise she got these days.

But he looked good. He looked like he worked out on a regular basis. He was tall enough, muscular enough.

"Are you staring at me for some particular reason?"

Oh no. Had she been staring at him the whole time while he was actually looking at her?

"What? I'm not staring at you," she said, brushing it off. He smiled slightly, completely aware that she was lying.

"Okay, whatever you say," he said, chuckling as he turned back around and looked at the water.

"You're awfully full of yourself," she said, crossing her arms.

"I'm not the one who was staring. Is it my chiseled cheekbones?" he asked, putting his hands on both of his cheeks and making a face.

"Yes, that must be it. They're awfully pointy."

"Pointy?" he said, reaching up again and touching one of his cheekbones. "I'll have you know, I've always been told I had magnificent cheekbones."

"Are you two really back there talking about your

cheekbones while I'm trying to teach you about crabs?"

Emma stifled a laugh. "Well, it's not exactly the most enthralling topic."

"Would you like it if I just shut up and take y'all out for a ride in the marsh?"

Heath and Emma looked at each other, each of them trying not to smile.

"Well, I mean it does feel a little bit like you're giving us a book report…" he said, sheepishly.

"Don't worry, it's not the first time I've heard that. Some people are just not into being educated," William said, laughing.

"It's actually a beautiful ride. I wouldn't mind just sightseeing a bit," Emma said.

William winked at them, a sure sign that he knew something was going on between them, and they wanted some quiet time in the back of the boat.

Emma didn't know what was going on. She just knew that she felt comfortable with him, and he seemed to enjoy her company. But, she was known for over complicating things in her mind, and this might be one of those instances. The guy might not be interested in her at all. Maybe he was just trying to make friends with anybody he could.

"So, what brought you to Seagrove originally?"

"I told you. I got a job running the lighthouse."

"What did you do before that?"

"Well, that's kind of part of the story I don't want to talk about," she said, softly.

"Sorry. I didn't mean to pry. Although…"

"What?"

"If we're going to be cooking together a lot, what are we going to talk about? Ingredients? I mean, I don't think either of us has kids, so that's out."

"I see. So it's deep dark secrets, ingredients, or kids? Those are the only topics? Why don't you ask me what my favorite type of music is, or what my favorite color is?"

"Fine… What's your favorite type of music?"

"Heavy death metal rap." He stared at her, his eyes as wide as saucers. Emma laughed uncontrollably. "I'm just joking! It's jazz. I really love jazz."

"I'm scared to ask any more questions."

"Okay, let me ask you a question. Why were you traveling around for so many years alone?"

He sighed. "Are you sure you want to know? It's kind of a sad answer."

"If you want to tell me, I'd like to know."

"My wife passed away three years ago."

"Oh, Heath, I'm so sorry. I shouldn't have asked."

He smiled slightly. "No, it's okay. It's just a hard

thing to think about, so I try not to, but it's impossible."

"What was her name?"

"Katherine. We were together for over fifteen years until cancer took her away."

Her heart ached for him. She could see the sadness in his face, and she couldn't imagine how hard it was to move on with life after losing the woman he loved.

"I'm really sorry for your loss."

"Thank you. After she died, I couldn't bear to stay at our house, so I sold everything I owned and went on the road. I'm an artist, and she loved sunsets. So I started traveling everywhere painting sunsets, mainly at beaches, and selling the paintings. For some reason, it just felt like the only way to stay connected to her because she loved seeing the sunset so much."

Emma wanted to burst into tears. She had never heard anything so beautiful in her life. What kind of man loved his wife so much that he would travel for three years straight just trying to stay connected to her through the sunset? It was poetic.

"I can't believe you did that."

"What do you mean?"

"I've never had a love like that. One where you

would travel to the ends of the earth to try to stay connected to the person you lost. I don't think I've ever loved anybody that much. How sad is that?"

He shrugged his shoulders. "It just means you haven't found your person yet."

"Do you think we all just have one person?"

"That's a deep question. It's one I haven't figured out yet. I guess I'll know one day. I will say I think every type of love is different. One isn't better or stronger than the other. Just different."

"Have you dated since she passed away?"

"Not really. I tried a couple of those apps, and that's definitely not for me. Having had what we did, I'm looking for something deeper than swiping across the screen and meeting up with a stranger."

She felt bad for being so attracted to him, like she was trying to take someone else's husband away. Even though his wife was dead, she could tell that he was still devoted to her. He might never be ready to date anyone, although he was definitely dating material. He was exactly the kind of guy she'd been searching for her entire life.

"Yeah, I've tried some of those apps myself. Really not my thing."

"Okay, guys, we're about finished. The dock is

just over there. I hope you enjoyed the ride," William said, a few minutes later.

They pulled back up at the dock, and Heath climbed out first, carrying his insulated tote. He turned around and reached down to help Emma out. A chivalrous thing to do, of course.

She took his hand. It was warm and strong, and she really didn't want to let it go but it seemed inappropriate to just try to hold his hand all the way back to her car.

"Thanks for the tour," he said, shaking William's hand.

"Any time. And if y'all ever want to learn the actual information about the marsh, come see me again," he said, laughing as he hopped back into the boat and started fiddling around with something.

"I had a good time. I'm sorry I made you tell me your deep dark secret."

He smiled, revealing two dimples. Dimples. A woman's kryptonite.

"It's fine. It's not something I should be hiding anyway. I guess I'll just have to find out your deep, dark secret when we start cooking together."

"Oh, I'm not one to give in so easily."

They started walking toward their cars. "Are you saying I gave in easily?"

"Well, I know your secret, and you don't know mine."

They stopped in front of her door. "Well, I guess I'll just have to live in the mystery for a while. I'm not the pushy type."

"This was fun. But, I'd better go. I have a bunch of kids coming to the lighthouse on a field trip tomorrow, and I need to prepare myself mentally for that."

"Yeah, I have a yoga class to go to. Janine said my quadriceps need work."

She waved goodbye to him as he walked up the sidewalk toward the yoga studio. There was still something so familiar about him that she couldn't put her finger on. It was more than just feeling comfortable around him. It was like she'd met him before, and she knew she hadn't.

~

JULIE STOOD outside of Colleen's front door. She knew she was home because she saw her car, but she couldn't bring herself to knock. She needed a few more moments to think about what she was going to say.

She and Dawson had had a long talk last night, and he had made her see that overreacting was only going to cause a rift between her and her daughter. She definitely didn't want that.

But, at the same time, she was hurt. She didn't understand why Colleen didn't trust her enough to tell her. And a part of her was sad that she had missed out on her oldest daughter's wedding, even if it was in Vegas at one of those tiny little chapels.

"Mom?" She turned to see Colleen standing on the other side of the flower bed, garden gloves on her hands. For a moment, she had a flashback when Colleen was a little girl playing in mud puddles in their yard back in Atlanta. She had always loved working outside in the dirt.

"Oh, hey. I was about to knock on the door."

"Is everything okay?" After Dawson had told her the news last night, he had called Tucker and asked him not to say anything. They wanted to give Colleen and Julie a chance to talk without Colleen realizing her mother already knew. It was all very confusing.

"Yes, everything is fine."

Colleen dropped her gloves on the ground and walked closer. "How is Madison?"

"Doing a lot better. Resting mostly today."

"Good. Come in, and we'll have some tea."

Julie followed her into the house, and walked

over to the kitchen, sitting down at one of the high barstools in front of the breakfast bar.

"I like the new paint," Julie said, pointing out the new light blue color Colleen had painted in her kitchen. It was a small space, but decorated very nicely.

"Thanks. Here you go," Colleen said, sliding a glass of sweet tea in front of Julie.

"Thanks, honey."

"You seem kind of down. Is everything all right?" Colleen asked, leaning against the counter with her forearms resting on it.

"I wanted to talk to you about something that happened yesterday."

"Yesterday? What is it?"

"Now, don't get mad at Tucker."

"What did Tucker do?"

"Well, he thought you had come to the bookstore and told me some important information."

Colleen's eyes grew wider. "I don't know what you mean…"

"He was trying to be traditional and chivalrous, so he went to talk to Dawson. And then Dawson came to the hospital and thought I knew."

She put her face in her hands and groaned loudly. "Nooo…."

"I have to say I was very surprised," Julie said softly.

Colleen put her forehead on the counter. "I'm so sorry, Mom."

Julie reached over and touched her arm. "Look at me."

She slowly stood up and looked at her mother, her face all scrunched up. "Do you hate me?"

"Of course not. It was just… shocking. I guess I assumed you'd want a formal wedding with your family, at least." She was trying so hard to maintain her composure and not cry or yell.

Colleen sighed. "I thought I did want that. When Tucker proposed, I was shocked. He hadn't intended to propose in Vegas. He was going to ask you and Dawson for your permission to marry me, as old fashioned as that is."

"So, what happened?"

"We finished the convention and had another twenty-four hours in Vegas. We went to this romantic restaurant, and then we went dancing. We talked about our future, we had some wine…"

"Ah, wine. That'll do it."

"Anyway, he had the ring on him, and as we were walking in front of these beautiful fountains, he got down on one knee. He told me later he was winging it because he'd had no intention of doing it there. He said it suddenly felt right, so he did it."

"That sounds very romantic."

Colleen reached across and took her mother's hands. "It really was, Mom. It was the perfect proposal for us. I hope you can understand that."

"Honey, I understand the proposal. What I don't understand is the marriage. Did you just not want your family at your wedding?"

"Is that what you really think?"

"I don't know what to think, Colleen." Julie stood up, nervous energy zipping around her body. "I always thought I'd be there when you got married. It was something I was looking forward to, and I think I'm just mourning that a little bit."

"I always thought you'd be there too, and I'm sorry you weren't. But, surely you can understand that people make decisions in the heat of the moment. I can't say I regret it. I'm glad I didn't have the giant wedding, honestly."

"It didn't have to be a big wedding. We could've had a small one. Or you could've gone to the justice of the peace, and then we could've had a luncheon."

Colleen walked around the counter and faced her mother. "We could have done those things. You're right. But we didn't, Mom. We got married, and I hope you can find a way to accept that."

Julie sucked in a breath and then blew it out. "I do accept it, honey. I'm happy that you're happy. I love Tucker, and I know how well he treats you. I just hate that I missed seeing you say I do."

Colleen smiled. "Wait! I have something. Hang on!" She ran out of the room and reappeared holding her cell phone.

"What are you doing?"

Colleen swiped around for a moment. "Yay! I found it!"

"Found what?"

"Come with me," she said, taking Julie's hand and leading her into the living room. She turned on the TV and pressed some buttons on her phone. "I just need to mirror my phone to the TV."

"I have no clue what that even means."

"It means I can show you this." She pressed one more button on her phone's screen and a video appeared on the TV. Colleen and Tucker were standing in front of a wedding officiant who looked more like Elvis than Julie expected.

"I didn't know there was a video."

"Neither did I, but I found it on the chapel's website. It's just a clip, I think."

They spent the next few minutes watching Tucker and Colleen say their vows, and Julie's eyes filled with tears. She reached over and took Colleen's hand as they watched. It wasn't the same as being at the wedding, but to see the look of love on their faces was more than enough for her right now.

When it was over, Julie took a tissue from the box on the end table and dabbed at her eyes. "Sweetie, that was just beautiful. I had no idea a little Vegas chapel wedding could make me so emotional."

"Now do you see why we did what we did?"

She laughed. "Not totally, but I get it. Sometimes, too much love overwhelms you."

"Like you and Dawson?"

She nodded. "Yeah, like me and Dawson. I'm glad you've found your dream man, Colleen. I know the two of you will build an amazing life together."

"Thanks for understanding. Well, at least a little."

Julie giggled as she pulled her daughter into a tight hug. Family was a funny thing.

CHAPTER 8

*E*mma ran around the house like a headless chicken, doing random tasks like fluffing the throw pillows on her sofa. Why was she suddenly so nervous about having Heath over to cook with her? This wasn't a date, she reminded herself. The man was still grieving over the loss of his wife, and it seemed he might never be available for another woman anyway.

Still, he was cute, and she was lonely. Might as well enjoy looking at him while she cooked.

"Knock, knock!" he called from the other side of the open screen door.

"Sorry, I didn't see you there. Let me take some of that." She opened the door and tried to take one of the grocery bags.

"No, I've got it." He turned slightly and walked past her toward the kitchen.

"You know, I am physically capable of carrying groceries. I run a lighthouse by myself, for Pete's sake."

He set the bags on the kitchen counter and smiled. "Can't help it. Chivalry and all that."

Emma rolled her eyes, but secretly thought how attractive it was when a man protected a woman. Maybe outdated to a lot of people, but she liked it. She'd never tell him, though.

"So, you got everything for chicken and dumplings?"

"I think so. Are you sure we need to make the dumplings from scratch? They had frozen ones at the store."

She scrunched up her nose. "Frozen? I don't think that makes us legitimate chefs if we use frozen."

"Oh, so now we're trying to become chefs? And then what? Open our own restaurant?"

Emma laughed. "Never say never."

"Yeah, well, I say never. I'll keep painting, and you keep..."

"Finish that sentence."

"I don't know what your official job title is. Lighthouse lady?"

She slapped his arm lightly. "Lighthouse keeper, thank you very much."

"Okay, but I think lighthouse lady has a better ring to it."

"I'm getting hungry. Should we get started?"

"Let's do it. Why don't I put on some music first?" Heath said, pulling out his phone. He found a jazz station and started it playing in the background.

"Nice. I love this song," Emma said, trying to keep from smiling at the gesture. "Okay, can you preheat the oven to three-hundred fifty degrees? I'll get the baking pan ready for the chicken."

"Sure." He walked over to the oven and pressed the bake button before setting the temperature.

Emma sprayed the pan with nonstick spray, coated the chicken breasts with oil, and sprinkled salt and pepper on them. Once the oven dinged, she slid it onto the top rack and set a timer for forty minutes.

"Let me take a look at the recipe," she said, walking over to the book she'd bought at the bookstore. "It says we should start the dumplings after the chicken is cooked, so it appears we have some time."

"It's almost sunset. Can we climb the lighthouse?"

She thought for a moment about whether she really wanted to climb those stairs after a long day of working, but he seemed so excited. "Let me get the keys."

They walked over to the lighthouse door, and Emma unlocked it, with her Walter following along underfoot as usual. He loved to climb up to the top, although she never let him out into the area where the railing was for fear that he might just jump off.

They didn't talk much as they climbed, mainly because it made pretty much anyone out of breath to get to the top. It was a lot of stairs, but she couldn't remember how many exactly. That was a part of the tour that she just eliminated. Nobody needed to know that exact fun fact, although if somebody asked her at some point, she would have to make something up.

"Wow. The colors from this view are amazing. Look at the pink over there," he said. It struck her that most men would never notice something like the colors in the sunset, but with him being an artist, it was the very first thing he picked out.

"It's beautiful. Sometimes I like to come up here in the evenings with a good book and wait for the sun to set. I drink a glass of wine or a cup of coffee.

Basically, I have a sad life sitting at the top of the lighthouse alone," she said, laughing.

"I don't think it's sad at all. I'd much rather spend time with nature than with people, to be honest."

"Really? You seem like you'd be a people person."

"Not really. I was always kind of shy, even as a kid. I loved to draw and read books. Doesn't exactly make for a happening social life."

"I was the same. I would read at least a book a week, and my mother would tell me I needed to get outside and play with the neighborhood kids. That sounded like the worst thing in the world to me. I didn't even have a bicycle until middle school when she forced me to get one."

"I used to ride my bike down to the creek and pick muscadines. I had a couple of little friends in my neighborhood. Tommy and Jason. They were cool kids, but I definitely wasn't. We weren't even friends at school. Just neighborhood friends."

"Times were a lot simpler back then."

"Yes, they were. I didn't have a lot of friends in school. I was way too shy."

"I understand. And making friends as an adult is even harder."

"Yeah, at least school is set up for you to socialize somewhat. Adulthood means you have to go out of your way to talk to people. And most of the time, I'd just rather paint or read or watch a documentary."

She smiled. "You like documentaries?"

"Don't judge me."

"I'm not! I love documentaries. Have you seen that one about the two sisters who didn't know they were sisters? And they ended up working at the same office?"

"No, I haven't seen that one. Sounds interesting."

"You'll have to watch it."

"Maybe we can watch it together," he said, softly to the point where she almost didn't hear him. She didn't respond because she didn't know what to say. Watching something together seemed a lot more like a date, and right now she was confused about what was happening between them.

"Well, we had better get back to the kitchen. The timer on my watch says we only have about fifteen minutes left. I think we can start prepping the dumplings now."

He nodded. "You're right. We should get back to work. Hey, do you mind if I come up here and paint the sunset one evening?"

"Of course. Just let me know when."

He smiled. "Thanks. I guess it's a good thing I know the lighthouse lady."

∽

JULIE FELT a little lonely in the bookstore without Dixie there as much as she used to be. She had sat Julie down and explained to her what the doctor had said and that she needed to take some time for herself to do things for her health.

Of course, Julie wanted Dixie to be as healthy as possible. She didn't want her stressed out about working, especially at her age. She should be relaxing, traveling, and doing whatever she wanted. She had earned the right.

Today, she was working on revamping a new section of the store for science fiction books. It wasn't exactly her favorite genre, so she didn't find herself thumbing through the books like she would if it were romance or women's fiction.

She heard the chime ring on the front door, and was thankful for the break. She put down the stack of books and walked up front only to see Tucker standing there, sheepishly looking at her.

"Hey," he said, not as verbose as he normally was.

"Hey. Is Colleen okay?"

"Yes. I think she's planting some new flowers in our front bed. I should be there helping her, but she told me to leave. She doesn't like to be bothered when she's gardening."

Julie chuckled. "That's very true. So, what can I help you with?"

"I came here to tell you how sorry I am about how everything happened. I never intended for it to go the way that it did."

"I know," she said, sitting down at one of the tables. She patted the area across from her, and Tucker sat down.

"I took something away from you that I didn't even think about at the time. I just felt overwhelmed by love for your daughter, so I hope that means at least a little something to you."

"I realize that now. I'm still a little sad that I didn't get to be there in person, but I was glad to see the video that Colleen showed me."

"Is there anything I can do to make it better?"

"Just take good care of my daughter. Be a good husband. She didn't exactly get to see a good example of that at the end of my marriage."

"I will always treat your daughter with the utmost respect. You never have to worry about that."

"Then that's all I can ask for. You don't need to feel guilty anymore. I'll get over it. It's not the worst thing that's ever happened to me," she said, laughing.

"I promise we won't keep secrets like that from you again. It was so hard for both of us, but especially Colleen. After we put the rings on our fingers, we realized what we had done. I hope you know it wasn't intentional."

She reached across the table and put her hands over his. "I know that. And I appreciate your apology, but it's really not necessary. I'm glad that my daughter has someone who loves her so much that he simply couldn't wait to marry her."

He smiled and looked down. "I do love her that much. I've never been so excited to spend the rest of my life with someone as I am right now."

"Then that's all that's important."

Tucker stood up and walked towards the door as Julie turned to go back to work. "Can I ask you something?"

"Of course."

"What do I call you now?"

"I mean, you've always called me Julie, so I guess you can do that."

"Well, it's just that I was wondering… I mean because I'm so close to you… can I call you Mom?"

Julie smiled broadly, her eyes welling with tears as she put her hand over her mouth. Swallowing hard, she responded. "I would be honored."

Tucker nodded his head and smiled. "Okay then. Have a good day, Mom." Without looking at her again, he quickly hurried out of the store, and Julie was glad about that because she felt a stray tear falling down her cheek.

~

DIXIE SAT down in her chair, and leaned her head back, staring at the ceiling. She was exhausted. The doctor had told her to relax and find some hobbies, but finding hobbies seemed to be the thing that was stressing her out the most.

In the last few days, she had tried learning pottery, going to one of Janine's yoga classes, and she had even joined one of those groups of senior citizens who walked around the local park. None of it seemed like something she wanted to do on a regular basis.

Dixie had always been young at heart. Even though her body was aging, her mind was still just as young as it had ever been. She made inappropriate jokes, she stayed up way too late, and she even found herself liking some of the younger music, although she would never tell Harry because he hated all of it. If it wasn't jazz, it wasn't music as far as he was concerned.

Still, she just didn't see herself becoming a potter or a speed walker. For the first time in a long time, she felt out of place. She was an old woman who didn't want to do old woman things. Her body was betraying her, but her mind was still sharp as a tack, even if it occasionally forgot some things.

Today, she was feeling awfully hopeless about her future. How was she supposed to keep mentally sharp and physically active if she didn't like anything that was available to her?

"So, anyway, Tucker came by the bookstore and apologized. He's just the sweetest man. I think Colleen is super lucky." Julie sat back down in the chair next to her. She had come over to check on Dixie, which made her feel good but old at the same time.

"He's a good boy," Dixie said, barely able to muster the words.

"Are you good? You seem awfully tired today."

"I've been trying all these new hobbies, and all they've done is make me exhausted and irritated."

Julie chuckled. "Not a fan of hobbies?"

"I'm not a fan of being an old lady. I guess I should just sit in my chair for the rest of my life doing large print crossword puzzles and petting a cat. I don't even have a cat. Am I supposed to get one now? I could be a crazy old cat lady."

"I don't think being older and having a cat necessarily makes you crazy."

She groaned. "I guess you're right. That was a lazy stereotype. I'm just in a mood today."

"The Dixie I know rarely gets into a bad mood, so something must be wrong. Do you want to talk about it?"

She reached over and squeezed Julie's hand. "No offense, hon, but you're young. You wouldn't understand. One day you will."

"I think you're putting too much pressure on yourself just because of what the doctor said. You should do the things that you enjoy, no matter what those are. It doesn't have to make sense to anybody else. What do you like to do?"

"I like to work. I like to feel needed and useful. I don't want to go walking around the park with a bunch of other old people, trying to stop the hands of time."

"You know, walking is good for you, though. If you don't like that group, find some other group."

"I don't like pottery.

"You don't have to do pottery," Julie said, laughing. "You have a great chance to find things that you want to do in your second act of life."

Dixie looked at her. "Sweetie, this is not my second act. This is more like my third or fourth act. I'm coming up on the closing scene, if you know what I mean."

"Don't you say things like that! Wasn't it you that told me you're as young as you feel?"

"Darlin', I don't feel young. My brain does, most of the time, at least. But this body is starting to get worn out."

"Okay, let's look at the problem. You're feeling tired. You feeling like your body is getting older. What can you do about that that you actually like?"

"Well, it sure ain't yoga or walking around that park."

"Tai chi?"

"Too slow.

"Karate?"

"Do you want me to break my hip?"

"Ballroom dancing?"

"That would give me vertigo."

"I'm running out of ideas," Julie said, laughing.

"Well, I have been thinking about one thing but it just seems so outlandish that I don't know if I could even pursue it."

"What is it?"

"This lady at the senior center told me about a new tennis team they're starting up. I used to play tennis back in my younger years."

"Well, I don't see anything wrong with that! Why can't you play tennis?"

"I have Parkinson's disease. What if I trip and fall?"

"You could trip and fall walking to the bathroom. All of us could. I would think it might help build up some muscles that you're going to need as you get older."

Dixie sat there thinking for a moment and then a smile spread across her face. "You really think I could play tennis?"

"Are other older women playing tennis?"

"Well, yes."

"Then I know you can. You're Dixie! You can do anything!"

Suddenly, she felt more hope than she had felt in weeks. Tennis had been something she loved as a teenager and young adult, and somewhere along the way she had let it go. Could she really get back to playing it now? There was a small inkling of belief deep in her spirit that told her maybe she could.

⁓

SuAnn sat across from the reporter, feeling a little bit of anxiety in her stomach but refusing to give into it. She wasn't one for anxious thoughts and feelings. As soon as she felt butterflies in her stomach, she imagined squashing them with her hand.

"So, we will begin shortly as soon as the camera is set up. Have you ever been on local TV news before?"

"No, I surely haven't. But I used to wanna be on TV when I was younger. I wanted to be one of those weather girls."

"You mean a meteorologist?" the young woman said, looking at her funny.

SuAnn waved her hand. "Oh poo! Back in my day, we didn't call them meteorologists. It was the weather guy and the weather girl. And the weather girls were always beautiful. Buxom, tighter fitting sweaters, for sure. But they got all the attention."

To that, the reporter didn't know what to say it seemed. She sat there quietly, a slight smile pasted on her face until the man with the video camera told her it was time to record the interview.

She was surprised when she got called by the TV station from Charleston. She didn't expect her little magazine article to gain her so much popularity, but her bakery had been packed with people ever since it came out.

She had even been called by a large company wanting to talk to her about putting her pound cakes in stores across the country. It was amazing, everything that had happened, and her head sometimes felt like it was spinning. Most people didn't get these kind of opportunities, especially in their older years, but she felt like she had some kind of new beginning.

"Okay, we're going to get started. If you'll just sit quietly until I ask you the question, and then my camera guy behind me here will be recording your answers."

"Let's get started then. I've got things to do."

Again, the young reporter stared at her for a moment like she didn't understand the language SuAnn was speaking. Still, she pasted on a big TV grin and began the interview.

"So, SuAnn, tell me how you started this bakery that has become so popular in the last few weeks."

"Well, I opened this bakery after moving here to be closer to my daughters."

"And where did you come up with the recipes?"

"When you're from the south, there's lots of old family recipes." The reporter waited a few seconds, like she thought SuAnn should talk longer, but she wasn't one for fluffy conversation. She was a "get to the point" kind of person.

"It seems like you've gotten really popular since the magazine article came out. How has that been for you?"

"Well, I suppose it would be good for anybody to have so much more business all at once, wouldn't you think?"

The reporter cleared her throat. "I would think so." SuAnn got the distinct impression that she was pretty new at this.

"I'm happy to have more people coming to try Hotcakes. And we have lots of other things besides just pound cake. I'm working on a new blueberry crumble that will make you want to slap your momma."

"I'm sorry?"

"You've never heard that term? Aren't you southern, sweetie?"

"Yes, I am."

"You gotta know your heritage, dear."

The reporter smiled sweetly. "That's wonderful. So back to the article. What has been the most surprising thing you've noticed since it came out?"

"I've gotten a lot more customers lined up in the

morning than normal. This is a small town, so we're not accustomed to so many people coming at once, except for tourist season. And then I've gotten calls from some big companies that might want to put my pound cake on the store shelves."

"That sounds exciting. Are you open to something like that?"

"Honey, if it makes me a lot of money, I'm open to anything."

The reporter stared at her for a moment, unsure of what to say and then smiled for the camera. "I'd like to say thank you to you for talking to us today. If you'd like to learn more about Hotcakes, make sure to check out our website. We'll have a link with contact information. Thanks for joining us. This is Amber Sutton for Eyewitness News."

A few seconds later, it was over. SuAnn thought she'd get a lot more airtime than that.

"That was it?"

Amber stood up quickly and picked up her bag. "That was it. Thanks a bunch."

Before SuAnn could say anything else, the news crew was out of the bakery, and she was standing there alone again. But she didn't care. She just got her face on television, and that was something she had always wanted to do.

CHAPTER 9

Meg sat in her car, staring at the building. She had only been working at the preschool for a few days, and already she wanted to go running and screaming into traffic.

As a mother, she felt terrible about it. How could she not want to spend all of her time with her little girl? And it wasn't really Vivi that was the problem. It was the fact that there were twenty-something other little kids in the room all the time.

She thought about all of those mothers over history who'd had ten or more children. How did they not lose their minds? She could barely sit through a session of coloring worksheets with five other kids at the table. She'd made a big mistake taking this job.

Still, she had promised Christian that she would try to stick it out for a while. They needed two incomes to support their little family, and she wasn't going to let him down.

She loved getting to see her daughter during the day, but maybe Celeste was right when she had said she didn't understand why Meg would take that job. She wasn't getting any time to herself. Morning, noon, and night, she was a mother. There was no downtime.

And, as it turned out, she needed some downtime.

A part of her felt like she was getting lost in motherhood. Maybe other new mothers went through the same thing, but she was losing who she was. She had forgotten the part of herself that just needed to be Meg.

But now she was stuck. She had taken this job, even though there were other candidates more qualified than her. The head of the school had hired her simply because her daughter went there, and she already knew the ins and outs of the school.

Now she was regretting it. She wanted a job that allowed her to just be Meg. Not mom, not teacher's helper. She wanted a job where she didn't have to wipe noses, break up silly arguments, and sing songs all day.

Suddenly, she was startled out of her stupor by somebody knocking on the window of her car. She looked up to see her sister staring back at her. Meg rolled down the window.

"Oh my gosh! You scared me to death!"

"Sorry. I just happened to be walking by, and I saw my sister staring glassy eyed at a building. I was afraid something was wrong."

Meg laid her head on the steering wheel. "Something is wrong. I took a job I shouldn't have taken."

"What do you mean?"

"My brain is turning to mush. I thought I would love being here with Vivi all day, but now I realize I'm not getting any time for myself. I'm losing my mind, and I'm losing myself."

"Sis, you're doing a great job. I'm sure all mothers feel this way at some point."

"I can't do it. I was supposed to be in the building ten minutes ago, and I can't seem to make my legs move."

"It's only been a few days. I'm sure things will get better."

Meg looked up at her sister. "Every day, we sing songs and color pictures. Kids pull things out of their noses and wipe them on my pant leg. It's not going to get better."

Colleen laughed. "Sorry. I didn't mean to laugh out loud."

"I have to quit this job."

"But what will you do?"

"I have no idea. My husband is going to hate me if I quit and leave us financially unstable."

"Christian adores you. He's not going to hate you. I'm sure he wants you to be happy no matter what."

She laid her head back on the steering wheel. "Do I really have to go inside?"

"Yes, you do. Where is Vivi, by the way?"

"I dropped her off up front. I'm supposed to park back here."

"Okay, you have to go inside and honor your commitment. Then you can figure out an exit plan. But you can't leave them hanging."

She sighed and then stepped out of the car. "Why are you so rational and reasonable?"

Colleen smiled and squeezed her sister's shoulders. "Because one of us has to be."

~

THERE WAS nothing Julie loved more than having lunch with one of her daughters. Colleen had invited her, probably because she still felt a little bit guilty about the whole marriage thing.

"I'll have a turkey club with potato salad," Julie said, looking up at the server. The outdoor café on the square in Seagrove was one of her favorite places to eat, especially this time of the year.

"I'll take the chicken salad croissant with potato chips." Colleen handed the menu back to the server.

"So Meg is unhappy at her job, huh? I hate to hear that."

"Yeah. She's had such a hard time figuring out what she wants to do with her life. I think it's safe to say that she doesn't want to be the teacher of little children."

"It's hard to parent adult children. I want to give my opinion, even when y'all don't ask for it. I want to guide you in the right direction because I have been through all of this, but I also know that you have to stumble and fall. You have to make mistakes to learn."

"Well she's definitely learning," Colleen said, laughing. Suddenly, she belched. "Oh my gosh. I don't know where that came from."

Julie looked around. "I don't think anybody heard."

"I've had the most unsettled stomach the last few days. Do you have any acid pills?"

"No, I don't carry them with me. Sorry."

"That's fine. I'm sure once I eat, I'll feel better."

"So, Tucker told you he came by to see me?"

"He did. He was feeling so guilty, but I think it really helped him to come talk to you."

"Did he tell you that he wants to call me Mom?"

"No, he didn't tell me that. That's so cute!"

"Yeah, it made me tear up a little bit."

Colleen smiled as she stared off into the distance. "He's the sweetest man."

"I'm so glad you two are happy."

"Thanks, Mom. Where's Dawson today?"

"He had to deliver a new breakfast table to Mrs. Lampkins, and then he promised to meet Dylan at school and have lunch. They let the parents do that once a month."

"Oh, that's neat. I'm sure Dylan loves that. How's he doing in school?"

"Much better. All A's and B's now. He went through some rough patches, but I think he's moving in the right direction."

"How is the festival planning coming along?"

"It's exhausting. I never knew so much went into planning a festival. Of course, I have help, but it's still stressful making sure everything is like it should be."

"It doesn't have to be perfect. Do you need any help?"

Julie shook her head. "No, but thank you. I know you're busy with your own business."

"Mom, let me help with something. I'm not that busy."

"Well, if you'd like to get some of the flyers hung around town, I wouldn't say no."

"Then that's what I'll do. Just give me a stack, and I'll get them handed out and hung up."

"Thank you. That will take a weight off."

"Okay, ladies, here's your food," the server said, walking up with both of their plates. She set them down on the table.

"Thank you," Julie said, smiling up at her.

"This looks good."

"Yes it does," Julie said, picking up her sandwich and taking a big bite.

Colleen picked up her chicken salad croissant and smelled it. "Does this smell funny to you?"

Julie leaned across the table and took a big sniff. "No, it smells the same as always."

Colleen brought it back up to her nose and

gagged a little bit. "Something smells off about this. It's making me feel nauseous."

"Do you want to send it back?"

"No. I think I'll just eat these potato chips."

"Honey, that's not a lunch. Let's just send it back, or get you something else."

"Maybe I'll just ask for a fruit cup."

"Are you good? You haven't been feeling sick lately, have you?"

"No. I'm just smelling things a lot stronger lately. Maybe it's because I haven't been used to being back home around all these smells."

Julie laughed. "What kind of smells does Seagrove have that other places don't have?"

"We're near the ocean and the marsh. When I was in Vegas, there were smells, but they were very different."

"I should think the smells in Seagrove are a lot better than the ones in Las Vegas, especially on the strip," Julie said, giggling.

"You're probably right about that."

"Are you eating this?" Meg asked, seeming to appear out of nowhere. She dragged a chair over to the table and picked up the chicken salad sandwich from Colleen's plate.

"No, it smells funny. Don't eat that."

Meg smelled it. "No, it doesn't. It smells fine. Can I have it?"

Colleen shrugged her shoulders. "Suit yourself. Just don't call me in a few hours when you're hunched over a toilet bowl somewhere."

"Meg, what are you doing here? Shouldn't you be at work?" Julie asked.

"We had an early day."

"Where's Vivi?"

"Oh, I ran into Dawson near the school. He took her for ice cream, and then they're going back to the inn so they can look for seashells at the beach."

"He's a good grandpa," Julie swooned.

"Anyway, I needed quiet time for mommy before my head exploded," Meg said, taking a bite of the chicken salad and moaning. "This is so good. You need to get your nose checked, sis."

"Colleen told me you're having… challenges… with your new job?"

Meg laughed. "Challenges? That's one way to put it. Mom, what I've learned from working at a preschool is that other people's children are living nightmares."

Julie laughed loudly. "But Vivi is perfect?"

She smiled. "Yes. Well, except at bedtime. Or if I ever tell her no for anything, ever."

"Maybe you just need to give it more time."

"No. I can't. I will need maximum strength mental health medications and possibly a straight jacket. I just can't. I spoke to my boss today, and she's going to call back the other applicants that were on the short list."

"And how does Christian feel about this?" Colleen asked, taking another chip from the bag.

"He knows I'm doing what I need to do. And Vivi didn't care. I don't even think she understood that I worked there."

"What will you do now?" Julie asked, taking a sip of her tea.

"Well, that's why I wanted to come find you."

"Me?"

"I heard through the grapevine that Dixie can't work as much?"

"Correct."

"Can I have her job then?"

"Wait. You want to work at the bookstore?"

"Not forever, but for now. I like to read, and I can talk to people. Plus, I've filled in there a bunch of times, so you don't have to train me."

"I mean, I do need the help…"

"Yay!" Meg said, standing up. "I'm going to go call Christian and tell him we won't have to move into a box under the bridge." Before Julie could say anything else, Meg was gone.

"She's awfully peppy today."

Colleen rolled her eyes. "Probably got into the candy at the preschool."

~

HEATH DIDN'T KNOW why he was so nervous. Emma was coming over to his house tonight so that they could cook stir-fry together. Asian food had long been one of his favorites, so he had picked a recipe that seemed easy enough but looked like it would taste good.

He wiped down the kitchen counters one more time, even though they weren't dirty. He had just moved into the place, after all. But for some reason he felt like he needed to impress her.

They got along well. They had fun together. But he still didn't know if she was leaning towards friendship, or she was interested in him. He didn't even know if he was interested in her.

After so many years of being with one person, he had a hard time imagining his life with someone new. And he had a hard time picking up on the signals.

Still, he couldn't allow himself to get too deep into the questions about whether dating Emma might even be a good idea because he had to focus. Focus on just the moment he had right now. Focus on cooking dinner. Focus on adjusting to a new town.

Maybe he was just lonely. Maybe he just longed for someone to talk to at the end of the day. His emotions were all jumbled up inside, and it would probably be a good idea to see a therapist, he thought. He wasn't going to do it, but it was probably a good idea.

Before he had too much more time to think, he heard Emma knock at the front door. He looked around one more time to make sure he hadn't left his underwear on the floor or something, and then he turned the knob.

"Welcome," he said. He immediately felt awkward. Why did he say welcome? Why didn't he just say hello or something?

"Thank you. Here, I brought you a gift."

She handed him something wrapped in plastic that smelled very good.

"A gift?"

"Like a housewarming gift?"

"Oh, I get it. I was afraid we were supposed to

exchange gifts. Come on in." He stepped back and opened the door, allowing Emma inside.

Whatever he was holding in his hands smelled good and sweet. But Emma smelled good too. That was very distracting.

"Nice place. Your view is great."

He laughed. "Not as good as the view from the top of a lighthouse."

He set the items she had given him on the kitchen counter and pulled back the plastic wrap to reveal what smelled like a delectable peach poundcake.

"From Janine's grandmother's bakery."

He nodded. "Hotcakes, right?"

"Yes. She thinks she's a celebrity right now because she got interviewed in a magazine and then on the local TV news. I'm pretty sure she's going to start signing autographs on the sidewalk any minute now," Emma said, laughing.

"Well, it smells great. I can't wait to have it for dessert. Care for a glass of wine?"

"Oh, fancy. Sure."

He walked over to the other side of the kitchen and picked up the only two wine glasses he owned. He bought them at a thrift store before moving to Seagrove.

He picked up the bottle of wine and carefully poured some for each of them, handing one of the glasses to Emma.

"I hope you like white wine?"

"I like *any* wine."

Heath laughed. "So, how was your day today? Anything exciting happen?"

"Well, I had a group of crazy little kids come to the lighthouse and drive me absolutely insane. One little boy snuck off and somehow locked himself in the lighthouse, so I had to run and get the keys. That was great."

"Wow! I bet he's fun to deal with at home."

"Every time I have a bunch of kids come to the lighthouse on a field trip, a little part of my biological need to be a mother dies," she said, taking a sip of the wine and leaning against the kitchen counter.

"I've always heard that you love your kids way more than you love other people's kids."

"Probably true. Let's just say I would never be a good teacher or daycare operator."

"Do you want to sit on the back porch? Watch the sun go down before we start cooking?"

She smiled slightly. "Okay."

They walked out onto the porch and sat down, facing the marsh. He loved the colors that he saw each evening. They rivaled any of the sunsets he had painted so far.

"Do you think you'll keep running the lighthouse forever?"

"I hope not. Don't get me wrong. I like my job a lot. But if I do get married one day and have a family of my own, I don't think it's feasible to live in a tiny cottage at the base of a lighthouse."

"Probably not. I mean, historically the people who live in lighthouses are typically loners, one would think."

"At the time I came here, I wanted to be a loner."

"Yeah? Has that changed?"

She puckered her lips and looked up like she was thinking long and hard about his question. "I'll say that I think it's changing. I'm not so raw now."

"I know you said you don't want to tell me your deep dark secret, but if you ever do, I'm not going to judge."

"You say that now, but if you knew what brought me here to Seagrove, you might not want to cook with me."

"I highly doubt that unless you're dangerous with knives?"

She laughed. "Not exactly. More like guns."

Heath froze in his seat. "Excuse me?"

"I guess you're going to find out no matter what. People in small towns like to talk, even if they're well-meaning."

"I'm sure the gossip mill runs strong."

She nodded. Emma stood up, one arm draped around her waist, the other holding her glass of wine as she stared out at the marsh. "I was a police officer, and I was forced into a situation where I had to take a man's life."

He didn't know what to say. "I'm really sorry you had to go through that."

She took a sip of her wine. "When I came to Seagrove, I was really messed up. I was second-guessing myself and everything I had done in my whole career. I was in a relationship I was trying to leave. It was just a mess."

"But you seem better now."

"You never forget it. I was just traumatized by the whole event. I know police officers are supposed to be able to handle stuff like that. I know it's part of the job that you might have to take a life. But when it happens to you, you don't know how you're going to react. I didn't take it well, and I ended up here as the lighthouse keeper."

He stood up and walked closer. "So how have you gotten better?"

"Therapy, for one thing. Making friends like Janine. Giving myself grace and forgiveness. It's something I have to work on every day. Even though it was justified, there's a family out there missing a member, and I'm responsible for that. I don't think I'll ever get over it, but I have learned to live with it."

He couldn't believe the type of strength she had. He had never met anyone who had taken a life, for any reason. He couldn't imagine what that was like to know that she was ultimately responsible, yet it sounded like it was justified.

"I can't begin to understand what that feels like, but it's inspiring that you have been able to get the treatment you need."

"Thanks. So, do you think any less of me now?" she asked, looking over at him.

He smiled slightly and shook his head. "Not at all. I actually think more of you. Now, if you mess up this dinner tonight, I will take off points for that."

Emma laughed loudly, accidentally snorting at the end. "Oh my gosh!"

"Did you just snort?"

She covered her face, which was turning red. "I haven't done that in years! My friends in high school used to call me piggy because I snorted so much when I laughed. I guess when I became an adult, I didn't laugh enough to do it."

"Well, then I feel very honored that I made you laugh hard enough to snort."

"You might be sorry for that."

"Are you ready to start cooking?"

"Yes. Just don't say anything funny."

CHAPTER 10

*J*ulie was exhausted after a long day at work. She just wanted to get back home, put on her snuggly pajamas, and take a nice long bath. The busy season was gearing up at the bookstore, and she was thankful for that, but sometimes she just needed to fall into her husband's waiting arms and get a good night of sleep.

Having the extra responsibility of planning the festival was also weighing heavily on her mind. She was enjoying it, and she knew people were going to love all of the activities at the festival. But, it was still a very tiring task to take on, especially given that Dixie had cut way back on her hours.

Now, Meg wanted to work at the bookstore, and

Julie had to admit she was relieved because she desperately needed the help.

As she pulled into the driveway of the inn, she let out a long breath and closed her eyes, leaning her head against her car seat as she turned off the ignition.

Home. There was just nothing like home.

For so many years, she hadn't always loved coming home. Even though she thought her marriage to Michael was still good when it actually wasn't, she had started to feel their relationship getting further and further apart during those last few years. Sometimes, she would pull into her driveway and dread what argument they were going to have that night.

Still, she kept it together because she had daughters, although they had grown up at that point. Still, a mother's heart feels guilt when she thinks about breaking up the family that her children have known. It doesn't matter how old they are.

Now, her girls had barely any relationship with their father, and that made her sad. He didn't know what he was missing out on. Grandchildren, marriages, fun family memories. It was his loss, but his daughters lost out, too, because she was sure they missed having a dad.

Of course, Dawson had stepped into the role very well. Colleen and Meg loved him, and they looked at him like a father figure, but nothing would ever replace their biological father. Sometimes, she even considered calling Michael on the phone and telling him the damage he was doing, but she decided against it. If a person couldn't figure out on their own that they were missing out, who was she to tell him?

"Are you going to get out of the car tonight?" She turned her head to see Dawson standing at the window, smiling and waving. She opened the door and stepped out.

"Sorry. I was lost in thought."

"I can tell."

She walked straight into his arms and pressed her cheek against his chest, her favorite place in the world.

"I love my job, but some days people try my patience."

"Oh yeah? What happened?" he asked, taking her handbag and slinging it over his shoulder, his other arm around her shoulders as they walked towards the front porch.

"I had one woman who wanted to order ten copies of a romance novel for her book club, but I only had eight. I couldn't make her understand that I can't have the books delivered to her within the next two hours if I don't actually have them in my possession."

They walked up the steps towards the front door. "That sounds reasonable."

"And then, one of the vendors for the festival had to pull out because his mother is sick, so now I have to find a totally different magician for the kids."

"And it's necessary to have a magician at the festival?" he asked, chuckling.

"It is if you've put it on all the flyers."

Dawson opened the door, and Julie stopped in her tracks. The living room was dark except for what looked like a million candles lit all over the room.

"Come on inside," he said, smiling.

"Dawson, what is all of this?"

"Well, I thought since my amazing wife was trying to make a wonderful, memorable event for everybody in town, the least I could do is make a wonderful memory for my wife."

Her eyes welled with tears. Maybe it was the romance of it all, but it might have also been the absolute exhaustion she was feeling.

"Really? You did this for me? Where is Dylan?"

"With your sister, learning to babysit."

Julie laughed. "I think we both know Janine is never going to let Dylan babysit."

"Are you hungry?"

"Always."

He grabbed her hand and pulled her toward the dining room door, pushing it open to reveal candles all over the table and a meal laid out. It was all her favorites. Country fried steak, mashed potatoes, corn on the cob slathered with garlic butter, home-made yeast rolls, and peach cobbler.

"What do you think?"

"I think I have the most amazing husband on the face of the Earth." She turned around and hugged him tightly, kissing him on the cheek.

"I'm going to go get the wine, so you just have a seat and take a load off."

He slipped into the kitchen as Julie sat down, happy to be off her feet. She kicked off her flats and wiggled her toes around.

She couldn't believe he had set all of this up for her. Sometimes, in the day-to-day happenings, it was easy to let marriage get stale. She knew that better than anybody. But Dawson always made the effort, and that was more than Michael had ever done.

"I can't believe you did all of this."

"You deserve it," he said, pouring them both a glass of wine. "Now, we can go ahead and eat, or we can do this." He pressed a button on his phone and suddenly music started playing. It was her favorite slow song to dance to. "Want to start with a dance?"

She nodded her head. "Of course."

As they swayed back-and-forth in their own dining room, Julie looked up at him and thought about how incredibly blessed she was to have a husband like Dawson. He was thoughtful, protective, and kind. Even on her worst days, she always had so much to be thankful for.

～

"You know what we need?" Emma asked, as she opened a can of bamboo shoots.

"What?"

"We need music."

"You mean like jazz?"

She thought for a moment, putting her index finger on her chin. "Actually, I would be down for some eighties pop hits."

He laughed. "Sounds like a plan. I have a little Bluetooth speaker over there on the coffee table."

Emma walked over and connected her phone to

the speaker, pressing play on her favorite playlist of eighties songs. The first one was a Whitney Houston song, and she found herself dancing her way back to the kitchen.

"Is this too loud?"

"What?" he yelled back at her, standing only a few feet away. Emma chuckled.

"I guess it was too loud. I love a good dance party while I'm cooking."

"I can't tell you the last time I had anything that I would refer to as a dance party," he said, stirring the rice.

Emma opened a can of baby corn, drained it and poured it into the rice mixture. "I get bored a lot being home alone so much. I'm pretty sure my dog thinks I'm insane, but I do a lot of dancing. While I'm getting ready in the morning. When I'm getting ready to go to bed at night."

"I'll have to be sure to look down the street and see if I can spy the silhouette of you doing pirouettes in the window.

She laughed. "I don't know how to do a pirouette. But I can do the moonwalk if I try really hard."

He turned and looked at her. "Oh, I'm going to need to see that."

"No way," she said, holding up her hand.

"You can't brag about knowing how to do the moonwalk, and then not do the moonwalk."

She covered her face with her hands. "I can't believe I'm going to do this." Emma kicked off her shoes, leaving only her socks, and turned sideways giving herself a good ten feet of space behind her. She lifted up her right foot onto the ball and then proceeded to moonwalk across the hardwood floor.

Heath clapped. "That was actually pretty good!"

"So, what secret talent do you have?"

He shook his head and looked back at the rice. "I have no secret talents. I know how to paint, that's about it."

She leaned against the counter and crossed her arms. "I don't believe you. Everybody has a hidden talent."

"Well, I don't."

"How is that possible that you're so artistically talented, and you don't have a hidden talent? Like, can you whistle really loudly? Do crossword puzzles at the speed of light?"

"Nope. None of that. Well…"

"What?"

"I can juggle."

"Juggling is a hidden talent! Let's see it."

"No, I'm cooking," he said, obviously trying to get out of it.

"I can stir the rice. It doesn't take a rocket scientist to do that. I want to see you juggle." Emma walked over to the fruit bowl and grabbed three small oranges, holding her hand out toward his.

"Fine. But you know you are very pushy," he said, laughing as he took the oranges. He closed his eyes and sucked in a deep breath like he was working up the nerve. Finally, he tossed the three oranges into the air and started juggling. When he finished, he bowed like he was on stage.

"Very nice! Very nice!" she said, clapping.

He put the oranges back in the bowl and returned to the stove top. "I'm sure that was quite impressive."

"It was."

For the next few minutes, they chatted and cooked, with music playing in the background. Tonight's meal was a vegetable stir-fry with a side of sesame chicken and homemade eggrolls. It was an intensive process to make everything, but when they finally sat down at the table, Emma was famished and happy to have so much food in front of her.

She turned down the music so they could hear each other talk during dinner.

"So, where did you grow up?" Heath asked as he poured each of them a glass of sweet tea.

"I was originally born in North Carolina, but when I was a kid we moved closer to family in South Carolina."

"What a coincidence. I lived in South Carolina for a while when I was a kid. What part were you in?"

"Near the Lowcountry. Just outside of Beaufort."

He furrowed his eyebrows. "That's really crazy. We lived there for a while, closer to the marsh land."

"Maybe we passed each other in the grocery store or something," she said, laughing as she took the first bite of one of the eggrolls. They were delicious, if she did say so herself.

"Maybe so. What made you decide to become a police officer?"

She shrugged her shoulders. "I don't know. I guess I wanted to serve and protect my community."

"That's a very noble thing to do."

"I guess so, but it didn't exactly work out for me."

"Maybe the universe had other plans for you."

"I hope so. Lately, I've kind of felt like my life was over." Realizing what she had just said, Emma put her hand over her mouth. "I'm so sorry."

"Sorry for what?"

"I shouldn't have said that. You lost your wife…"

"Emma, you don't have to walk on eggshells around me. I didn't think anything about what you just said. I'm just enjoying having this conversation."

"You are?"

"Yeah. It's been a long time since I've been able to just relax and talk to somebody. I spent three years running around the globe trying to outrun my emotions."

"It didn't work?"

"It worked in the sense that I was able to avoid the grief. It would hit me at quiet times, of course. But I took out all of my emotions in my paintings. I didn't speak any words about what I was feeling. I just let the paintings speak for me."

"I haven't seen any paintings in this house. Why don't you display them?"

"I sold a lot of them through my agent, and I only kept a few. It seems kind of weird to display my own paintings," he said, laughing, before taking a bite of sesame chicken.

"If I had that kind of talent, I would wallpaper my house in paintings and charge people five dollars to come inside and look at them."

He laughed. She liked to hear him laugh.

"You say that, but I don't think that's true."

"Can I see some of your paintings?"

She knew that was being pushy and presumptuous, but she still hoped he would say yes.

"I have a couple in the guest room. I guess I could go get them."

"I mean, if you don't want to share that with me, I understand. I'll pay you five dollars," she said, smiling.

"I tell you what, I'll let you see them for free this one time," he said, leaning in a little closer to her across the table. For some reason, that gave her a little shiver down her spine she wasn't expecting.

Heath got up from the table and walked down the hallway. A few moments later, he returned with two large canvases facing him.

"Are you sure you don't want the five bucks?"

"I'm sure," he said, looking a little nervous. "Don't make fun of them."

"You're a professional artist. I'm pretty sure they're going to be better than anything I could ever think of doing."

"I don't know why I have an easier time selling them in an art gallery than I do showing somebody I just met."

"Maybe that means my opinion has more weight than a professional art gallery?" she said, laughing.

"Okay, this first one was done off the coast of California. This was about six weeks after my wife died." He turned the painting around, and Emma's breath left her body. It was the most beautiful painting of a sunset she'd ever seen.

She said nothing but stood up and walked closer to it, putting her face within inches of the painting and staring at all of the colors. Sure, she could see pink and orange and a little purple. But it was the shades in between she wasn't expecting, the way he mixed the paint to make it look so realistic. It reminded her that life isn't just about the bright colors, but about those shades in between where life isn't so bright.

"Heath, this is beautiful. It literally took my breath away to see it. I can almost feel the emotion coming through the painting. I'm not an art person usually, but I can actually *feel* this painting. Is that weird?"

He smiled. "No, it's not weird. That's actually a wonderful compliment."

"Can I see the other one?"

"This one was done off the coast of Florida, on the Gulf. It was one of the most unique sunsets I've ever seen. I wasn't having any particular feelings when I painted this one, but I kept it for some reason."

He turned it around, and Emma was blown away. It was even more beautiful than the last one. It had hints of a dark sky mixed with pink, yellow, and orange. It was like the sunset was bursting out of the darkness.

"I love this one even more. It's just so beautiful and different."

He's pushed the painting toward her. "It's yours."

"What? No! I could never take something like this."

"I want you to have it. Seriously. I'm never going to hang it up because, like I said, that would be weird to me. It deserves to have a good home where someone loves it."

"You should sell this. I'm sure you could make a lot of money on it."

"I kept it for a reason, Emma. It was such a unique sunset, and I just felt weird about selling it. I can't explain it. Maybe it's because it was meant to be with you."

Her heart was pounding in her chest. This felt like a very heavy, turning point kind of moment. A part of her wanted to walk around the painting and hug him tightly, and try to take away the last three years of pain he had been feeling.

"Are you sure?"

"Totally sure."

She took the painting from his hands and stared at it for a long moment, trying to will herself not to cry. It was one of the nicest gifts anyone had ever given to her.

"Thank you. I will cherish it for the rest of my life."

He smiled and then walked back to the table and sat down. "That's all an artist can ask for."

She carefully leaned it against the back of the sofa and walked over to the table, sitting down and wiping one stray tear off her cheek. "Thank you, again."

"You don't have to thank me, Emma. I'll rest easy tonight knowing that painting will always have a good home."

They continued eating and chatting, but all Emma could think about was where a man like this had been all her life. Even if he only turned out to be her friend, which was the way it was looking, she considered herself blessed to know somebody like Heath.

CHAPTER 11

*A*s Julie worked on the bookkeeping for the month, she was surprised to see a very spry Dixie come flying through the door.

"Wow! Don't you look cute?"

Dixie was wearing a hot pink tennis skirt, a white polo shirt, and one of those bedazzled sun visors. She looked like she belonged in some sort of south Florida retirement community.

Dixie slowly twirled around, being careful not to fall over from her balance issues. "I think I look pretty snazzy myself!"

"Did you have your lesson this morning?"

"I did, and I have to say my tennis instructor is pretty easy on the eyes. His name is Javier."

Julie laughed. "Oh, is that so? Did you tell that to Harry?"

She waved her hand. "Lord, no! What he doesn't know won't hurt him."

"I have to say, this is the Dixie I remember from the day we met out on the sidewalk. You seem so much happier."

"You know, I am. I loved running my bookstore and working here with you, but I needed something new and different. Getting out there and playing tennis this morning showed me that I can do a lot more than I thought I could. Sometimes I think when we get older, we just sort of buy into the thought that we can't do anything anymore. And that's just not true. There were lots of older people there today."

"I'm so glad to hear that. You deserve only the best," Julie said, walking over and hugging her.

"And I intend to have it! You got time for lunch today?"

Julie sighed. "This festival is going to be the death of me. I need to go meet with the people who are going to supply the bouncy house for the kids. Then I have to go hand out some more flyers. Colleen is helping me, but we have a lot of them."

"Honey, give me a stack. I don't mind helping out."

"You're supposed to be taking time for yourself, not doing my dirty work."

Dixie snatched a stack of the flyers. "Well, I have them now. You can't take them away from me, or that's elder abuse."

"Oh, you're a sly one, Dixie."

As she waved and walked toward the door, Julie felt such happiness for her. Everybody deserved to live a full life until the day God called them home. Dixie finally seemed like herself again, and it was a lovely sight.

~

COLLEEN BRUSHED her hair and stared at herself in the mirror. Maybe it was the exhaustion of all the travel she'd done in the last few months, but she didn't look like herself. She didn't even feel like herself.

She would have to make an appointment with her primary care physician soon, because she needed her energy for the next few months as they continued to build their business and start out on their journey as a married couple.

She put on more foundation and used more concealer than she'd used in a while to eliminate the dark circles under her eyes. For some reason, she hadn't been sleeping well lately. She couldn't get comfortable, and she kept having to pee all night long. Was this what getting older was going to be like? She wasn't even out of her twenties yet!

She quickly brushed her teeth, and tapped her toothbrush on the side of the sink before putting it up. She was in a hurry to get to the festival. Her mother would need help to make sure everything went off without a hitch, and it started in less than an hour.

"Are you about ready?" Tucker asked as he walked into the bathroom.

"I think so. I really want to take a nap instead, but I promised Mom I would be there to help her."

"Are you sure you're not coming down with something?" he asked, putting his hand on her forehead.

"I don't feel sick. I just feel worn down. I don't know what's going on."

"Maybe you should stay home tonight."

"I'm going to the festival. Now, are you still going to be my date, or do I need to find somebody else?" she teased.

"I'm always going to be your date," he said, putting his hands around her waist from behind and resting his chin on her shoulder as they looked in the mirror. "Does it feel different to be married?"

"Yes, but in a good way. What about you?"

"I couldn't be happier to be your husband," he said, kissing her on the neck. "I'd better get going. I promised Dawson I would help him get the stage put together. They have a bluegrass band coming for part of the night."

Colleen laughed. "Yes, because nothing says romantic dance music like bluegrass."

Tucker left, and she finished putting on her make-up before turning to walk out of the bathroom. Something made her turn around and stop in her tracks. The sight of a pregnancy test on her bathroom shelf. She bought one, for reasons unknown to her, just to have in case she ever needed it.

Without thinking, she grabbed the box and slipped it into her handbag. Something told her she might be taking that test sooner rather than later.

～

HEATH STOOD there on the beach, staring into his wife's eyes. How could she be there? She left him three years ago. God had taken her home, and yet here she stood looking at him with those hazel green eyes of hers.

"You have to listen to me, honey. There's going to come a day when you'll meet a woman who will steal your heart again. Don't let her get away."

"But I don't want to be with anyone else. I want to be with you."

She reached up and put her hand on his cheek, something she'd often done over the course of their marriage. "We both want that, but it simply can't be. You have way too much love in your heart to spend the rest of your life alone."

"But how will I know when it's the right woman?"

She smiled sweetly. "You'll know."

Suddenly, she was gone. Like a puff of smoke, she disappeared into the air. He turned in every direction looking for her, wanting just one more moment. Just one more word. But she was gone.

The next thing he knew, he was sitting up in his bed, struggling for air. His heart was pounding. He quickly flipped on the lamp next to the bed and searched the room, but she wasn't there. Realizing it had all been a dream, he felt a sense of loss all over again.

Heath looked at his watch and realized he'd fallen asleep when he was supposed to just take a quick nap before the festival. It was still light outside, but his room was darkened by the shades.

He jumped out of bed and quickly ran to put on his shoes. Even though he hadn't planned on going to the festival originally, he figured it would be a good way to get to know the town and maybe meet more of his new neighbors.

Still, the thought of the dream he just had weighed on his mind. Was it real? Was his wife really there to talk to him? What would she think if he started dating again?

Sometimes, the guilt plagued him. It felt wrong to stand in front of a church full of people all those years ago, pledging his love and loyalty to her for the rest of his life, and then going to date someone else. He had taken those vows very seriously.

But then there was that pesky part that said "till death do us part". Death parted them. Did that mean it was okay for him to finally start dating? And did he really want to?

If he was honest with himself, the time he had been spending with Emma was starting to affect him. He looked for her when he was walking down the sidewalk. He hoped it was her every time his phone rang. Those were the feelings of a man who was falling for a woman. And it made him feel terribly guilty.

With Katherine, he had known immediately that they were meant to be together. With Emma, it was different. It was slower, but strong. And he still didn't know if she was even interested in him that way.

Why did it all have to be so complicated?

～

"ARE you sure you don't need help with anything?" Janine asked for the third time. Julie was running around like a chicken with its head cut off, and Janine had been trying to help her since she got there. Her sister was like this, though. She didn't take help easily, and she was a multitasker to the nth degree.

"You have a baby in your arms," Julie said, rearranging stuff on one of the tables. They were giving little gift baskets to each of the people when they arrived. It had some brochures for local stores, samples of items at the bakery, handmade soaps from one of the vendors, and a bunch of other stuff.

"I'm not an invalid. I can just give Madison to William."

"I think William is helping Dawson assemble the stage."

"At least let me finish putting stuff in the baskets!"

Finally, Julie looked up at her. "Okay, fine. If you insist. These candles need to go in each of the baskets."

Janine walked over and started taking candles and putting them into each of the baskets while she held Madison in her other arm. It didn't take long for her to get down the skills of multitasking with a baby on her hip.

"Okay, the stage is ready. Tucker and William helped me, so we got it done quickly. The band should be here any second," Dawson said, walking into the tent, ducking his head down so it didn't hit the top.

"Can you go check on the parking situation? I want to make sure none of those orange cones are blocking the spaces behind the pharmacy."

Dawson saluted her. "Yes, ma'am! Come on Tucker, we have things to do." Tucker followed along like a little puppy.

"Where is Colleen?" Janine asked.

Julie looked around. "I haven't seen her. I guess she's not here yet."

"And Meg?"

"She's helping Mom in the bakery tent. You know, the town's new celebrity?" Julie said, laughing.

"Let her have her time," Janine said, wagging her finger at Julie. "Who gets to become a local celebrity in their seventies? I mean, without doing something illegal to get you on the news. And I think both of us worried that one day Mom would do something that would get her on the news in a bad way."

"Here, let me take her," William said, walking into the tent and taking Madison from Janine's arms.

"Thank you. She looks small, but she's quite heavy when you're holding her in one arm."

"I'm always happy to hold my little girl," William said, looking down at her. Sometimes, it made Janine's heart feel like it was going to burst when she saw how William interacted with his new daughter.

It was just so special to watch her husband, a man who had been so difficult to deal with when they first met, become the father to their daughter. He was a natural, and it warmed Janine's heart to see him so happy and content holding Madison.

"What else needs to be done?" Janine asked.

Julie finally stopped running around for a moment. "Honestly, I don't know. I think my brain is shutting down."

"Take a deep breath through your nose, hold it for a few seconds, blow it out your mouth."

Julie did as she was told. "That feels a little better."

Janine walked over and put her hands on Julie's shoulders. "Sis, you've done a great job. Everybody is going to have a fantastic time, and most of that is because of you. Stop putting so much pressure on yourself, and enjoy the fruits of your labor."

"I know you're right. You know I'm a bit of a perfectionist."

"A bit?"

～

COLLEEN STOOD in the bathroom of her grandmother's bakery. Maybe she was hiding, or maybe she was just scared. She stood there staring at the pregnancy test box, knowing that there was no way she was pregnant.

She had been taking birth control for many years because of heavy cycles. But there might have been some time on her "honeymoon" in Vegas where she forgot. There was wine involved, and she just couldn't remember.

She and Tucker had talked about waiting to have kids until they could afford to buy a bigger home. They had talked about all the things newlyweds talked about when it came to having children. They wanted them, but they also wanted to be "financially stable" first.

So she stood there, unsure if she should waste a pregnancy test or just go to the festival and try her best not to fall asleep.

She didn't feel overly nauseous or anything. Wasn't she supposed to have morning sickness if she was pregnant? She knew she could ask her sister, and even her mother, but she didn't want anybody to know. Even Tucker.

She was probably just being overly cautious. There was no way she was pregnant that quickly after getting married. Many of her friends had struggled with infertility or problems conceiving, so she just didn't see how it was possible that she could get pregnant so easily.

Of course, her sister sure did.

"Are you okay in there?" her grandmother asked from the other side of the door. Colleen had slipped by earlier, and she thought it had gone unnoticed.

"I'm fine, Grandma. Just a little upset stomach. Is somebody waiting for the bathroom?"

"No. Just wanted to make sure you didn't keel over or something." She heard her walking away, and she let out the deep breath she'd been holding.

Her grandmother was like a bloodhound. If something was wrong, she would know it soon enough. Colleen looked down at the pregnancy test one more time, and ripped open the box without hesitation.

She just needed to know. Maybe the symptoms were the beginning of a flu, or maybe she was just worn out.

Or maybe she was pregnant.

She quickly read the directions and then did what was required to take the test, before setting the test stick on top of the box on the counter. Now it was just time to wait.

~

As the festival got into full swing, Julie finally had a chance to relax. She was so glad that everything was going off without a hitch. There was nothing better than being able to see a job well done.

Her favorite part of the festival so far had been

the live band that was playing under the pavilion. They had hung twinkle lights everywhere, and it was a truly magical sight to see all of the couples slow dancing, and the kids twirling around to the faster dances.

They started with a bluegrass band, and some of the older folks really enjoyed that. Later, they had a country band that played classic hits, mainly from the eighties and nineties. Julie enjoyed hearing some of those songs.

"You did a great job, honey," Dawson said, walking up and putting his arm around her shoulders.

"Thanks. But, if it's all the same to you, I'm going to let somebody else handle this next year."

He laughed. "I don't blame you. How about next year we take a vacation during this time instead of almost driving you to the brink of insanity."

She pinched him on the side. "I think I handled it pretty well."

"You wanna dance?"

She thought for a moment. Her feet were hurting, and she really wanted to take a nap, but when else would she get a chance to dance with her handsome husband under thousands of twinkle lights in the middle of the town square?

"Absolutely."

He took her hand and led her out onto the dance floor, and they moved slowly to one of her favorite songs from the past. She wasn't a huge country music fan normally, but the old stuff really made her remember times long ago.

"This is a great festival," Celeste said. She hadn't even noticed that she was dancing with Ben right next to them.

"Thank you!"

"It looks like you did a lot of work. I'm sure you're ready for a break," Ben said, smiling.

Julie nodded. "Let's just say that I would never want to be an event planner. I will leave that job for somebody else."

"What are we talking about over here?" Abigail said as she and Griffin appeared on the other side of them. They were such a cute couple. They were newly dating, and Griffin was well known in town as being the new veterinarian.

"We're talking about all the work that Julie put in to make this festival a success." Celeste said.

"Oh yes! There is so much to do here. Have you done the dunking booth?"

"I think I'll avoid that one," Julie said, laughing.

The three couples continued dancing, and Julie

pressed her cheek into Dawson's chest, closing her eyes. She felt dead on her feet, and she wanted to go lay down, but the night had turned out to be magical, and she was going to just soak it all in while she could.

~

HEATH WALKED DOWN THE SIDEWALK, still unsure of why he was going to this festival. After the dream he'd had, he wanted to stay home and bask in the feeling of being near his precious Katherine.

It was a hard thing to love someone who had died. His love for her was always going to be there, but he didn't know if that meant he wasn't allowed to love someone else. Did loving someone else diminish his love for her? Was it a betrayal?

He wondered if the dream was real. Did Katherine really come to him and say those words? Or, as was more likely, did she say the words he wished she would?

He didn't know what he felt about people coming to him in a dream. He wasn't sure if that was real or just what people wished would happen. Sometimes, he thought his grandmother came to him in dreams.

He had been close to her as a child, and it always gave him peace when he had one of those dreams.

Right now he wasn't feeling very peaceful. He felt conflicted, sad, and uneasy.

Up ahead, he could see the pavilion lit up with twinkle lights and couples dancing beneath them. A part of him really wanted to do that with Emma. The other part of him felt like the most terrible person on the planet that he would hold another woman in his arms when he still loved his wife so much.

"Hey there." He turned to see Emma leaning against the front of the bookstore.

"Are you hanging out on the streets now?"

She laughed. "I'm pondering."

"Pondering what?"

"Going to the festival."

"Why wouldn't you?"

She blew out of breath, her cheeks poking out like a puffer fish. "There's a lot of couples up there."

"And you don't like them?"

"No, it's not that. I like all of them. Sometimes it's just hard being the only single person in town."

He walked closer and leaned against the building next to her, both of them staring out toward the square. "I know what you mean. Being new here, I don't know anyone, and it seems like everybody is coupled up."

"I was thinking about going back home, putting on my pajamas, and digging into a giant vat of ice cream."

"It does sound like an intriguing idea." They stood there quietly staring at the dancing couples. "Or…"

"Or what?"

"Well, the idea of going home and giving yourself diabetes in one night is appealing. I have to give you that. But there is another option."

"And what's that?"

"We could go to the festival together."

"Like a date?" she asked, slowly.

"I mean, we don't have to label it. We are just two single people who are choosing to go to an event together."

"Like a date," she repeated, but this time not in the form of a question.

Why was he having such a hard time calling this a date? "Sure. I guess we can call it that."

"Or just two friends?"

"Okay. We can call it that."

Emma threw her hands in the air and faced him. "I can't do this anymore!"

He was shocked. "You can't do what?"

"Can you make a decision?"

"A decision on what?"

She lightly knocked on his head like she was knocking on a door. "Hello? Is anything going on up there?"

"Did you drink wine before you came here?"

"Heath, can I be honest with you?"

"Yes, of course."

"I don't know what we're doing here. I can't tell if you want to be friends, or if you want something more. I've never spent so much time with a guy and not known what was going on."

He ran his fingers through his hair and leaned back against the wall again. "I don't know what I'm doing."

"I can believe that," she said, laughing.

"I haven't been with a woman in a very long time who wasn't my wife. I met her in college, and we got married right afterward. I've not done a lot of dating. The only other girlfriend I've had was way back in fifth grade, and I don't think that counts."

"I'm not trying to push you into something. Please know that. But I am a very black and white person. Maybe it's my cop training. I just need to know where this is going, even if we haven't gotten there yet."

"I've been wondering the same thing. I don't know what you're thinking either."

"I like you, and I would be interested in being more than friends."

It was the first time she said anything like that. It wasn't that he was surprised, but yet he was. He'd always assumed it, but then he kept second-guessing himself.

"Wow. That was upfront. Thank you for that."

"So I guess the only question is how do you feel?"

He stood there quietly for a moment and looked back up at the town square. "I guess I would just like to ask if I could have a dance?"

Emma smiled. "You know I like to dance."

He jutted out his arm and allowed Emma to lock hers through his. They began walking up toward the music, and he had never been more nervous about anything in his life.

CHAPTER 12

*C*olleen walked toward the pavilion, feeling completely shellshocked. Her pregnancy test had shown positive. She still didn't understand how it was possible.

Now, she was just wandering around town like a lost zombie. If she saw Tucker, she wasn't going to be able to contain herself. She wasn't even sure if she was excited or scared or just plain blown away. Her emotions had not bubbled up to the surface yet.

"Hey, sis. If you're looking for Tucker, he went to help Dawson with something. Is everything all right?"

"Yeah, I'm fine," Colleen said pasting on a smile. Of course, she was totally lying.

"Good. I've got to go find Christian and Vivi. She was getting her face painted."

"Okay, I'll just see you later."

She watched her sister run off to go find her husband and daughter, and she realized that she was going to be doing similar things as a new mother soon.

A mother. She was going to be a mother. Some-body was going to yell Mom, and they were going to be talking about her!

She thought about her own mother, and how she had done such a good job with Colleen and Meg. She had worked so hard, was always involved in their school, and kept them on the straight and narrow.

How would she be as a mother? Was she ready for that? Ready or not, she was going to be a mom soon.

She suddenly realized just how scared Meg must've been when she found herself pregnant with Vivi. Until now, she hadn't really understood what that felt like.

But with her fear and shock also came excite-ment. She was going to get to carry a baby, and a lot of women didn't get that blessing. That was not going unnoticed by her.

She was going to get to raise a child with Tucker,

and he was going to be the most amazing dad ever. He was a toy inventor! Who better to raise children with?

The closer she walked to her family and friends, the more relaxed she started to feel. She had a community around her. She wasn't alone. She would never be alone. That was a secure feeling to have, and she was grateful.

"Are you okay?" her mother asked, walking toward her. Now she felt conflicted. She had kept the marriage a secret from her mother for so long, and she didn't want to do that again. But she also didn't think it was right to tell her mother she was pregnant before she told her own husband.

"I'm fine. I've just been feeling a little tired today. I was looking for Tucker. Do you know where he is?"

"I know he was with Dawson earlier, but Dawson is back. Wait, I think I see him over there. Looks like he's helping out with the dunking tank."

Colleen nodded. "I'll just go have a chat with him, and then I'll be back."

"Okay, but let me know if you need anything."

As she walked toward her husband, she wondered how she was going to tell him. She had seen so many of those social media videos where wives did extraordinarily creative things to tell her husbands that they were pregnant.

She was *not* that person. There was no way she could keep this to herself more than the next fifteen minutes. She wanted to tell everybody, and that was mainly because she hated keeping secrets. It made her stomach hurt.

"There you are! I was looking for you earlier. Where'd you go?" Tucker asked.

"I went to the bathroom at the bakery," she said, pointing back behind her. "Do you have a minute?"

"Yeah, just let me tell Marcus he's going to have to run the booth alone for a little while." Marcus was the custodian at the local high school, and everybody loved him. He was loud and boisterous, and he was the perfect person to run a dunking tank.

A few moments later, Tucker met her over at one of the park benches near the pavilion. She made sure they were behind a tree so her family didn't come over and eavesdrop on their conversation.

"Is everything good?"

She turned to him and took both of his hands. "I need to tell you something."

"You're scaring me."

"I don't quite know how to say this without putting

you into complete shock, so I'm just going to come out with it. The reason I was in the bathroom is because I was taking a pregnancy test, and it was positive."

Tucker sat there staring at her like he didn't understand the language he was speaking. His mouth hung open slightly, and she was afraid he might actually start drooling at any moment. "Pregnant?"

"Yes. We're going to be parents."

She was trying to talk softly, but it was hard given all the music playing around them.

"But I thought you were taking some kind of pills?" It was just like a man to not even know they were called birth control.

"Well, I was. I've taken them for years. But we were in Vegas, and I might have forgotten a time or two. I'm sorry."

He stood up and paced around for a moment, and she was afraid her mother would see the spectacle and come running over there to find out what was wrong. "I'm going to be a dad?"

"It looks that way."

"And you're going to be a mom?" he said, pointing at her like he was trying to piece together how family trees worked.

"Again, I'm sorry. I know we were going to wait…"

"No, don't be sorry!" he said, sitting back down quickly and putting his hands on her knees. "This is the best thing I've ever heard in my life!"

"What? Really? But I thought you wanted to wait until we were financially secure and all of that stuff?"

"Everybody says that, Colleen. And nobody ever does it. Why should we wait?

"Well, we don't exactly have a choice about waiting now," she said, laughing.

"We're going to do this. We're going to be great parents. We're going to teach them to be good people. We're going to take them on fun trips. We're going to give them the best toys that any kids ever had."

"I'm so glad I get to do this with you," she said, tears rolling down her cheeks.

"And I promise, whatever weird pregnancy cravings you get, I'll get you the food. I don't care if it's octopus or ginger salad dressing or hot fudge sundaes with anchovies on top. I'll go out in the middle of the night, and I'll buy you whatever you want."

Colleen laughed and hugged him tightly. Everything had been a whirlwind lately. Engagement, marriage, pregnancy, all within the span of a few weeks. Her head was spinning, but she was so thankful for the way things were working out.

~

HEATH HAD FORGOTTEN what it felt like to have a woman in his arms. When he and Emma got to the pavilion, they talked to everybody, said their hellos, and then waited for a slow song.

She smelled good. Her hair smelled like a mixture of strawberries and vanilla, two things he liked very much.

It felt odd to have his arms around her. He remembered what it felt like to have his arms around Katherine, but this was a new feeling. Foreign, but good.

He was still at odds with himself inside. Was he supposed to feel guilty? What was wrong with him if he didn't feel guilty?

Getting therapy or going to grief counseling was sounding like a good idea right now, but it was a little too late. He was already falling for Emma. He had to admit that to himself. There was no way around it.

She was everything he was looking for in a

woman if he ever chose to be in a relationship again. And right now, it felt like he was choosing that.

He wasn't one of those guys who wanted to go out on dates with dozens of women. He didn't want to go out to clubs on the weekend or hang out in bars. He wanted to find a good woman he loved, and he wanted to build a life with her.

Emma was the first person he'd met that he found interesting enough to even entertain those kinds of ideas.

She had her arms wrapped around his neck, her face pressed close to his shoulder. Her perfume kept wafting up into his face, and he kept getting chills down his spine.

Was this how it felt to fall in love? It sure seemed familiar to him.

"Are you okay?" she asked, pulling back and looking up at him.

"Yes. Are you?"

She smiled. "I am more than okay. But I'm not the one who's grieving."

She knew him. She understood that she wouldn't be the only woman in his life. Katherine would always be there in the background. He would love her no matter what. But did that have to keep him from loving someone else?

"It feels a little strange."

"Tell me more about that."

He laughed. "Oh, are you my therapist now?"

"If that's what it takes. Otherwise we're just going to keep meeting at each other's houses cooking dinner for the rest of our lives."

"Would that be so bad?"

She giggled. "Yes, it would. Sometimes I'd like you to take me out to dinner at a restaurant. Or even dancing. You're pretty good at it."

"You know, if we get into a relationship, my wife will sort of be a part of that."

Her face looked more serious, and she nodded her head. "Don't you think I know that? Katherine was your true love. And she will always be your true love. But I just happen to think that people don't get only one true love."

"So, not just one soulmate?"

"I don't think so. That would be very sad if a person lost their soulmate young, and then they were destined to spend the rest of their life without love. I refuse to believe that's the way God wants it."

She didn't say anything else but instead pulled him closer and put her head back on his shoulder. Maybe she was right. Maybe there was some kind of arrangement where Katherine could still be there, guiding him and loving him from heaven while he loved another woman on earth.

~

COLLEEN AND TUCKER walked hand-in-hand towards the pavilion. This was one time that she was not going to keep a secret from her mother. She had learned her lesson already. So, they headed towards the pavilion where Julie and Dawson were slow dancing along with everyone else.

"Hey, Mom?" Colleen said, tapping her on the shoulder.

"Oh, hey, y'all. What's up?"

"We need to talk to you and Dawson. And can you grab Meg also?"

"Is everything all right?"

"Yes. Everything is fine. We just need to have a little family chat right quick."

Julie nodded and jogged off to get Meg. They met them under the tree just outside of the pavilion area.

"What's going on?" Meg asked, trying to hold onto Vivi who was attempting to wriggle away to get closer to the bouncy house.

"Well, Tucker and I just have some news, and we didn't want to keep any more secrets."

"Yes, let's not do that again," Julie said.

"Well, I don't know how else to say this, so I'm just going to blurt it out. We're pregnant."

Julie's eyes got wide as saucers before a huge smile spread across her face. "I'm going to be a grandma again?"

"Yes!" Colleen said, smiling and jumping up and down. Julie pulled her into the biggest bear hug.

"Was this planned?" Meg asked, laughing.

"No, but when one drinks a little too much wine in Vegas and forgets to take prescription medication, things can happen."

Everybody laughed. "Well, that just means this was meant to be. God had other plans for you two," Dawson said, hugging both of them.

"I'm scared to death, but I'm excited."

"Excuse me, but we're *both* scared to death," Tucker said, laughing.

"Everybody is scared when they have children. You think you won't have what it takes, or you'll screw them up. You'll figure it out, and you have all of us to help you," Julie said.

"Thank you. Now, if y'all don't mind, I really want to go home and go to bed. This explains all the exhaustion I've been feeling."

Julie hugged her one more time. "Go get some

rest. You're going to need it. In fact, rest as much as you can, because the rest of your life is going to be about that kid."

~

HEATH WAS surprised that his boxes were finally delivered. He had been waiting for the last set of boxes for what seemed like decades.

He had them all stacked up in the living room on the coffee table, and he was going through them little by little. Some of them brought on a lot of feelings and memories, like the wedding album he'd forgotten he had.

He spent most of the morning looking at those photos and wondering how to know if Emma could be the next love of his life. Would he call her his girlfriend? At his age, was that what you called the woman in your life? He felt so out of practice.

As he dug through the boxes, he came across some old school yearbooks. He had them going all the way back through elementary school. A lot of schools didn't do yearbooks in elementary levels, but his did for some reason.

He started with his high school yearbooks, looking up friends he had lost contact with over the years. He made a list of names that he could look up on social media to see if he could reconnect. He needed friends. He needed to get back to living his life.

Then he went down to his middle school years. Boy, was he a nerd. He wore thick glasses, had early acne, and for some reason his mother dressed him like he was going to join the circus. It was no wonder he didn't have a lot of friends in middle school.

Hours went by as he sat there looking and reminiscing, reading the comments his friends wrote in his yearbooks. There were so many good times that he had forgotten, and he needed to remember those. They brought a smile to his face.

Finally, he saw his elementary school yearbooks. He picked up the one from fifth grade and started combing through it. There was only one person he wanted to see in that yearbook, and it was his girlfriend from fifth grade. Besides Katherine, that was the girl he had loved most in the world.

He remembered her as being so nice to him when everybody else wasn't. She had been going to the school for a while before he came. Nobody else would talk to him or even sit beside him on the bus, but she did. She was just as nerdy as he was.

They both loved history, and they were two of the few members of the history club. Being a member of the history club got him bullied quite a bit, but he kept going because he liked spending time with her.

Her name was Janie, and until he met his wife, she was the prettiest girl he'd ever seen. She had long brown hair that she kept in two braids, and her eyes were the color of chocolate fudge with hints of gold. He remembered staring at her when they would sit together at the lunch table, and chasing her around on the playground at recess.

Finally, he worked up his nerve to ask her to be his girlfriend right before summer time. They had spent the whole school year together, and it took him that long. She said yes, and he felt the happiest he had in his whole life.

They spent part of the summer together, riding their bicycles and going to the creek. They would even sneak a kiss or two, although neither of them knew what they were doing. He remembered it fondly as a time in his life when he felt totally accepted by someone.

And then everything got shattered apart when his dad got relocated yet again. He found out he was going to be moving before the end of summer, and he had to tell her goodbye. They promised to write to each other, but it never happened. They were in fifth grade after all. But he'd never forgotten her.

He turned the pages until he finally saw her picture. Funnily enough, he still saw her as beautiful. He still looked at her just like he did when he was in fifth grade.

But something about her looked familiar. Heath looked closer at the page, staring into her eyes. Was that Emma?

~

EMMA WAS DOING HER LAUNDRY, one of her least favorite things to do. But it was that day of the week, and if she didn't do her laundry she would be walking around wearing foul smelling clothes and gathering cats from the local wooded areas.

She threw the last load in the washing machine and started it before she heard someone banging on her front door. That was unusual. Nothing like that ever happened in Seagrove.

Even though she still had a gun, she kept it locked in the safe. She didn't like to use it. It brought back a lot of bad memories. But if she had to, she would.

The banging continued. She finally walked closer

to the door, sliding behind it and peeking through the drapes. It was Heath.

"What are you doing? You scared me to death!" she said, opening the door and holding her hand to her chest.

"Janie!" he shouted, holding up a book. She feared that he had lost his mind.

"Who is Janie?"

"You?"

"What?"

"Did you go to this school?" He handed her the book. She looked at the front cover and recognized the name.

"Yes…"

"In fifth grade, did you go by Janie?"

Suddenly, she felt like she was made out of stone. Her body was frozen. "Oh my gosh, I did. From first through fifth grade, I went by Janie. My full name is Emma Jane."

"You don't remember me?"

"You've always looked a little familiar to me."

"Back then, I didn't go by Heath. People would make fun of me and say I was a candy bar. I know, it doesn't make any sense. Kids are dumb."

"What did you go by?"

"I went by my first name. David."

Suddenly, like a flood, the emotions almost overtook her. She was looking into the eyes of her childhood sweetheart. That little boy that she'd fallen in love with who had to leave when summer was over.

As silly as it seemed, she had never forgotten him over all the years. He was her first "love", and there were many times she wondered what would've happened if he'd stayed. Would they have grown up together and gotten married one day? It was a fantasy she had played out millions of times in her mind. How had she not recognized him?

"David?"

For reasons she couldn't explain, she stepped forward and hugged him tightly, not wanting to let him go. Slowly, he put his arms around her waist and they just stood there hugging.

"You remember me?" he asked in a whisper.

"Of course. I guess I just didn't put it together because the name didn't match."

They finally separated. "Same," Heath said, laughing. "Who would've thought we both changed our names? It's not like we were in the witness protection program."

She backed up and allowed him into the house, and they both went to sit down on the sofa.

"I stopped going by Janie because I told my mom

that the only person who was allowed to call me that anymore was you."

His mouth dropped open. "Really?"

"I cried and cried when you left. I was just a little girl, and I had no control over you leaving. I hated it."

"So we were childhood sweethearts? That's just crazy. How did we end up on the same little island on the same little street?"

Emma smiled. "Well, there are two theories I have. Number one, total coincidence. I don't buy into that one, by the way. The other one? I'm not sure you want to hear it."

"I want to hear it."

"Maybe Katherine orchestrated this."

He nodded. "I thought about that. I don't know what I believe happens after someone dies, but I want to believe that she led me to you."

"I guess the question is do you still have room in your heart for me?"

"Emma, I've been falling for you since the moment I met you. I just didn't want to admit it to myself because I felt so guilty. But knowing that you were my childhood sweetheart even way back then means that something is pushing us together."

"It seems that way."

"I have a question for you."

"Okay."

"Do you think it's possible to fall in love with someone without ever kissing them?"

She smiled slyly. "Absolutely not. Kissing is an extremely important part of falling in love. I mean, what if you kiss like a lizard?"

"I'll have you remember that we did have a few stolen kisses down by the creek."

"You were in fifth grade. What if your methods have changed? I really feel like I need to check that out before I commit to anything."

He slid closer to her on the sofa and leaned in, pressing his lips to hers. When they pulled back, they both smiled.

"That felt like coming home," he said. And that was all she needed to hear.

EPILOGUE

*H*e sat on his porch, staring out over the marsh. The sunset tonight was yet another beautiful one. They all were. Even watching thunderstorms rolling in over the blowing grasses was something to behold.

Although he had always painted sunsets, or at least for the last three years, he'd branched out into painting other things now. The lighthouse. Thunderstorms. The town square.

Since moving to town two months ago, his life changed completely. He could've never imagined all of the wonderful things that would happen to him after moving to Seagrove.

Not only had he reconnected with the first love of his life, Emma, but he had started painting again and selling those paintings in galleries around the country. He had also started teaching art lessons in town, and it was giving him great happiness to teach children and adults the art of painting.

But the best thing that had happened to him was Emma, by far. They spent almost all their time together, when she wasn't giving lighthouse tours. Knowing that she had been his childhood sweetheart felt like it meant they were supposed to be together.

At first, it had been a little hard. He had to admit that. He would always miss Katherine, but now he knew that she would want him to move on. It wasn't an accident that he came to this tiny little town, this dot on the map, and ran into the other woman he loved so long ago. Well, she wasn't exactly a woman in fifth grade.

They'd had so much fun reminiscing about their time in elementary school together. They had so many memories of racing their bikes, looking for tadpoles in the creek, and going to history club meetings together.

He was thankful that he moved away that summer because it allowed him to meet Katherine and spend all of those wonderful years together. And now he was thankful that he was able to reconnect with Emma for the second half of his life. God had truly blessed him twice.

"Coffee?" Emma asked, walking up behind him. She held one of his favorite mugs, made of thick pottery, in front of him.

"You know me well."

She sat down next to him, as she did every evening, to watch the sunset. Tonight, he really wanted to paint this one but he refrained. Sometimes he could get a little frantic with his painting and do it all the time, shutting out those around him. He vowed not to do that.

"How were your lessons today?"

"They were great. I had this little girl, I think ten years old. She has a lot of talent. I can't wait to see what she does."

"That's wonderful."

"How about you?"

"I have some news."

"Oh yeah?"

"I have decided to open a side business."

"A side business? What kind?"

"You know I love the lighthouse, and I'm going to continue to run it. But I feel like I need something else. Something to make me feel like I'm contributing to society."

"Okay…"

"I'm going to become a private investigator. I have the skills for it, and I know I can help people."

He smiled and reached over to touch her hand. "I think that's great, Emma. You're so smart, and I know you'll do well at this."

She smiled back. "Thank you. You're always so supportive."

He would support her in anything she wanted to do. His plan was to spend the rest of his life with her, even if they hadn't gotten engaged or talked seriously about marriage. No matter what, he wasn't letting her get away again.

"So, what should we cook for dinner tonight?" They had continued cooking together several nights a week, and they were both pretty skilled chefs at this point.

"I'm actually going to make Caesar salads, corn chowder, and grilled chicken with balsamic vinegar glazed brussels sprouts."

"That sounds really good. We'd better get started, right?"

She nodded. "We probably should. Can I ask you something?"

"Of course."

"Are you happy?"

"Immensely," he said, rubbing his thumb across her cheek. Are you?"

"More than I've ever been."

"Let's go cook, Janie." Occasionally, he brought out her old name, because it was only theirs. Only he called her that.

"All right, *David*. Let's get to it."

As they walked into the house, Heath thought about how fairytales could be real. Life wasn't perfect, and neither were people. But this ending, which was really a new beginning, felt very much like a fairytale.

～

WANT to read my other books? Visit my website at www.RachelHannaAuthor.com for a complete list!

Come join over 10,000 other readers in my fun Facebook reader group! https://www.facebook.com/groups/RachelReaders